THE A... UNTHINKABLE . . . AND TOTALLY UNEXPECTED. IT CHANGED THEIR LIVES—FOREVER.

AMALIA—Living with the memory of her dead lover . . . sleepwalking through a stagnant marriage. War stripped away all pretense. She would never take anything for granted again . . .

DANIEL—A devoted husband, a respected civil servant . . . not even Amalia suspected his double life, the hidden secrets of his heart . . .

AVI—An Israeli expatriate. He thought he had lost his love for his homeland—and for Amalia . . .

JULIE—Avi's American wife. Repelled and attracted by Israel's fierce energy, would she always be an outsider?

LIEB—A wealthy New York surgeon, he gave more than money. In time of need, he gave himself . . .

AN UNKNOWN SOLDIER—In a country where no one is anonymous, he lay unconscious and alone, burned beyond recognition, his mysterious past the missing link in the fragile chain that bound them all. . . .

Books by Yaël Dayan

NEW FACE IN THE MIRROR
ENVY THE FRIGHTENED
DUST
DEATH HAD TWO SONS
SINAI DIARY

THREE
WEEKS IN
OCTOBER

Yaël Dayan

A DELL/ELEANOR FRIEDE BOOK

TO DAN AND RACHELI

CONTENTS

THREE
WEEKS IN
OCTOBER

Rarely does the holiest of Jewish holidays fall on a Sabbath. A wise enemy seeking a favorable date to attack a Jewish state would surely not miss this coincidence. Israel is paralyzed on Yom Kippur. All communications are shut down, airports are closed. Like a big heart suffering an artificial lapse, the whole country is at a standstill. Late Friday afternoon people crowd the synagogues, offering a prayer of atonement, and then they go home, many to fast, but all to avoid activity of any kind for twenty-four hours.

On Saturday, October 6, 1973, the holy silence was broken. The radio network started operating about noon, sounding codes for draftees and reservists to join their units. Men in uniform entered the synagogues with lists of names in hand, and traffic began to move again all over the country. By 2 P.M. the Yom Kippur War had started.

Massive Egyptian forces crossed the Suez Canal into the Sinai peninsula, and Syrian armor, in numbers unknown in this area before, broke through the thin defense line on the Golan Heights.

History has recorded many things that happened on this day and on the days of bitter battles that followed. The whereabouts of cabinet ministers and division commanders have been reported, the size of the armies involved, the number of tanks and aircraft and manned divisions. A footnote may even comment on the weather, a bright, cloudless day, warm and pleasant. Historians try to understand how an army famous for its intelligence branch could be taken by such complete surprise.

What happened to most of the people is not recorded in history books. Their sorrows and actions and failures and hopes are generalized into such statements as "The mood at that time . . . ," "The overall feeling was . . . ," "Mainly the people were . . ." The actual details are buried in individual memories. Occasionally they come to the surface, stained with emotional patches which distort whatever objective truth lies in personal histories.

History written without the perspective of time hurried to define this war as traumatic. It was as if an earthquake had shaken the country; it would never be the same after those days of fighting. Analysts claimed it was not only a group-shock affecting the state and its ruling institutions, but equally relevant to each individual living there. Men, women or children—they would never be the same again, having lived through this war. The individuals portrayed in these pages, though all fictitious characters, may shed some light on that judgment, for their story is told during the three weeks of the Yom Kippur War.

PROLOGUE

Daniel and Amalia Darom dressed to go to the neighborhood synagogue. They were not religious, but thought it was part of their duty as parents to attend services on Yom Kippur with their two sons. The little boys, Ofer, five, and Rani, three, excited at the prospect of an "outing," were ready and waiting. They all left their fourth floor apartment to walk the three blocks. To an onlooker they seemed like an average family from a statistics manual. Daniel Darom was slightly taller than his wife, hair cut short to hide a few silver streaks. A civil servant in the ministry of finance, ex-military, he had retired a colonel at the age of forty to begin a civilian career. Amalia was an attractive woman with a worried face which made her rare smiles even brighter. Not beautiful, but young looking and noticeably tidy. Daniel wore a checked jacket over an open-necked shirt; Amalia's uniform on occasions like this was a blue skirt and a matching turtleneck sweater. All members of the family had auburn hair and hazel eyes and were slim without being sportive.

The synagogue was crowded with worshipers.

Daniel took Ofer with him and Amalia carried Rani. Kol Nidre, the opening prayer, was sung first in whisper, again louder, and for the third time with unique excitement. The music was moving, but the words seemed meaningless to Amalia. The real meaning lay in the body of believers swaying, repeating, communicating. She was an outsider, not jealous, not envious of the faith they had and practiced, but just an awkward onlooker. They walked home from the service chatting casually. Was it hypocritical not to fast or even believe, and yet attend a service where other people openly revealed themselves, recited their sins and hoped to be pardoned?

Amalia hated the imposed silence, Daniel found it relaxing. At home they had a light meal and the children were soon asleep. They made love, a Friday night routine, quietly because of the children. Lovemaking was satisfactory to both, if somewhat mechanical, a friendly act rather than a burst of desire.

On Saturday morning it was Daniel who prepared breakfast for everybody, and then he took the boys out for a walk. When he returned, he tuned the radio to a local station where to Amalia's surprise codes of army units were being announced. He calmed her, or tried to, and explained that apparently there was going to be another war. That day. Maybe any minute.

Daniel called Beni, a commander he had served with in the past, and learned from his wife that he had left the house during the night. A call for Daniel informed him that he was to report at an Economic Emergency Center within an hour. Amalia felt like talking but couldn't. She managed to prepare a lunch before her husband left. At 2 P.M. the alarm siren was sounded. She took the boys and a blanket and walked quickly down the stairs with the other tenants to the underground shelter where the radio informed everybody of the beginning of a new war. The all-clear alarm came soon. The way back to the apartment seemed very long to her, as if she carried a heavy burden. Once inside she called her mother. She then called a surgeon she knew in the military hospital, and reached him in the orthopedic ward preparing the emergency section and evacuating civilians. Yes, he was sure they could use volunteers, especially during the nights. Many doctors were called to join their units, male nurses too. Could she call him later? If any of the rumors were true, they would need all the help they could get.

Amalia's mother had been a widow for a few years. She lived in a two-room apartment near the Yarkon River in Tel-Aviv, and worked in a public library five mornings and three afternoons a week. On Friday night, having refused to join her daughter and son-in-law, she brought her dinner tray to bed and listened to a B.B.C. concert. On Saturday she cleaned the apartmemt, though to any eye but her own it would seem spotless, and planned to read a seven-hundred-page book. Her son, Boaz, a couple years younger than Amalia, was with some friends up in the Galilee and she knew very little of his whereabouts or motivations. Her life since the death of her husband was more like that of a spinster than a widow. When

Amalia called with the news and offered to come and fetch her, she refused. She had lived through many wars, and for all she knew this could be a false alarm. The first thing was not to panic, she assured her daughter, and returned to her thick volume. When the siren was sounded she didn't go to the shelter, but turned the pages of her book with a touch of nervousness.

Avi Goldin decided to treat himself to a Chinese meal in London. It was the eve of Yom Kippur, but it didn't mean much to him. He was on vacation, halfway through a thesis he was hoping to complete for his Ph.D., and not really enjoying the leave. London was shabbier, drearier than he remembered it, the fun gone from King's Road and Chelsea, and he thought of flying to Paris the next day. The Chinese Dumpling Inn still served a decent meal, but there was little to do afterward. Avi was an Israeli who had moved to New York with his parents. He planned vaguely to return "home" one of these days, but praised himself on his "international" existence. Countries, states, nationalities didn't matter when you were deep in science.

On Saturday he slept late. His hotel bed was comfortable, and he ordered breakfast to the room. He turned on the radio and heard the news. In fifteen minutes, all theories forgotten, he was packed and riding the elevator down to the lobby. In another five minutes he was in a taxi on the way to Heathrow, a slow ride with the Saturday traffic in that direction. He pushed his way closer to the crowded El Al counter, flinging down his blue passport, explaining to the clerk that he was an officer and had to join his unit immediately.

"So does everybody," the clerk assured him and took his name. "We hope there will be a flight today. It may be the last one for some time."

Julie Goldin spent the weekend with her daughter, a girl of six, and her parents in Springfield, Massachusetts. The Rowes owned a pretty cottage. The kitchen was a relaxing green, Julie's bedroom pink and yellow, the den rust and olive green. They went to church on Sundays, barbecued on Saturdays and read *The New York Times* and *The New Yorker*. Julie played tennis and rode well; the only flaw her parents could find in her was her marriage. The Rowes had no Jewish friends and didn't know it was Yom Kippur, but after the barbecue on Saturday someone called to chat on the phone and mentioned that once again there was war in the Middle East. Julie's heart did skip a beat. Israel was the birthplace of her husband, and although they were separated, he was the father of her daughter. She called her in-laws in New York who assured her Avi was in London and there was no reason to worry. She'd know more when she got the Sunday *Times* the next day, she thought, and left it at that.

Dr. Leibowitz, a young-looking middle-aged plastic surgeon with a good practice in New York, had no qualms when he heard the news on October 6th. He packed his bag, threw in some instruments and hailed a cab to Kennedy Airport. If it's what they say it is, he said to himself, I could be of use. For years he had been avoiding the U.J.A. and Israel Bond dinners, thinking a contribution should be real, personal, not just a check. He even entertained thoughts of moving to Israel, if it grew to be more sophisticated, less pretty. He felt very heroic and important talking to El Al's station manager, explaining why flying him would add to the war effort. He didn't get on the first flight but he camped in the terminal and waited for the next one. He could never forgive the Arabs for having the chutzpah to launch an attack on Yom Kippur. In the German concentration camps the Nazis had given him extra food on that day, knowing he wouldn't touch it.

General Beni left for division H.Q. in the south on Friday night. His wife couldn't believe her eyes. "Driving an army vehicle on Yom Kippur? You'll be stoned to death!"

"Better than being shelled to pieces. The whole thing looks fishy and I am not going to be caught pants down, not even in a synagogue with a prayer book." He made a few phone calls and told his meek and understanding wife not to worry. It might be a false alarm, but if it weren't he'd better be in the right place. A short, stocky man, he didn't fit the silhouette of a winning hero, but he had all that it took. Quickness of decision, integrity, humor and a great love for everything he was sent to defend. He had a son in the army and his daughter was out studying with a friend, so he brushed his wife's cheek and mumbled something. She could hear the squeak of the wheels—the only car in the area moving that night—and then the sound disappeared and she wiped an unwanted tear. She was thinking of her son.

A lodger in Beer-Sheba had been locked up in his room since the fast began. He was fasting, but if he were praying he did so in the privacy of his little room.

It was a habit with him not to eat on Yom Kippur, wherever he was. He did write though, and filled a few pages of his diary. Toward noon he settled down to read a thin red volume reread many times. A knock on his door made him jump. His landlady informed him of the news, and offered him a radio in case his unit was called. He thanked her. There was no need. He put a few items into an old army bag, added the red book and a shaving kit, and left the diary in a drawer.

The traffic on Beer-Sheba's main street was the same as any other day. Trucks and private cars moved east, and a long line of hitchhikers, some in uniform, some in civilian clothes worn to services that day, formed at the exit to the city. The lodger joined the line. He wasn't going anywhere in particular. He didn't belong to a unit, but he was going to war and he was sure to find one. A large truck loaded half the queue and he pushed his way into it, settling in a corner on the cold metal floor.

The Rabbi in the small synagogue next to the central military hospital realized something was wrong. For an hour now people had been leaving, murmuring, whispering. There weren't many young faces as it was, but the few he was proud to have on Yom Kippur left in a hurry. Very solemnly Professor Rothman, head of plastic surgery in the hospital, left too, accompanied by his son-in-law.

Rothman looked like a professor, bespectacled, dressed in a dark suit, his prayer book bound in leather. He wanted to tell the Rabbi what was happening, but knew he'd find out soon enough. The general director of the hospital walked in and asked the Rabbi for permission to say a few words.

"A state of emergency has been declared. All doctors and other hospital staff are required to report to the wards. We'll give more information as soon as we have it."

Rothman walked home and changed his clothes, while his son-in-law borrowed his car and went to change into uniform. The Professor was not easily excited, yet he was uncomfortable. He didn't like surprises, good or bad, and his steps to the hospital gate were heavy and measured. There was so much to do, and so little time—if any at all.

BOOK ONE

Amalia

CHAPTER 1

For six nights I had been on night watch in Ward L of the central military hospital. The war was almost over, the broadcasts said, and finding it difficult to face the days, I arrived here with sunset and spent the night. In the daytime I slept, believing it helped time pass faster. I was an untrained volunteer and the services I gave were minor. The commotion during the day was great, the nights were peaceful yet never silent. Two nurses and a doctor dozed in the doctor's room. Watching infusion bottles, counting the drops, I felt like a spy looking at sedated bandaged soldiers fast asleep. I listened to the raindrops and a faulty tap dripping in the ward's kitchen.

The patients in Ward L suffered from burns. Most of them were armor soldiers caught in burning tanks. During the day their wounds were treated—skin grafts and heavy pomade, special baths and surgery. A team of physicians formed a human computer. They did the charts, measured the fluid output and ordered the blood tests. They controlled the high-protein diet and watched out for the slightest sign of infection. A team of surgeons worked around the clock in six operating rooms removing dead tissues, slicing circular full-thickness burns and dressing the burned tissues with pigskin bandages. They grafted skin which was rejected, and grafted again until the cells rebuilt and the patient's own skin could be used for more grafts, permanent ones.

Those with second degree burns moaned or cried in pain. They looked forward to the change of dressing when, like children, they are put in the bathtub till the bandages separate from the flesh and float about. Then a thick spread of silver sulfadiazine, white and soft, calms the wounds. They are bandaged and returned to their beds and to the drips of glucose or blood transfusions. They counted the hours until the next change of dressing. At night they were like babies in diapers attached to infusion tubes, static, seemingly painless.

Three people were asleep in the armchairs in the waiting room. Lea, whose husband had been brought in two days ago. He was still fighting for his life, a third degree case. He feels no pain and surgery fights bacteria, while she is a witness to the battle. She felt like an outsider, afraid to talk to the doctors, afraid to think or cry. A presence holding with enormous strength to an unpromised hope.

Bundled in an army blanket was Rina. I knew she was watching me in her sleep, and I looked back at her. Her young son had been brought in with a burned hand and a missing finger and would be leaving the ward tomorrow for a rehabilitation center. She and I will be separated again, perhaps for good this time. Our story dates back to another war, a man killed in battle—her husband, my lover.

It was long past midnight. The rain stopped and I warmed up the stale black coffee. The doctor was snoring lightly. The nurse, red-eyed, smiled and sipped from her plastic cup. We tuned the radio louder; it was always on. We talked about our children, wondered whether they'd remember this war, whether our absence at night affected them. We shared a tender smile, we ran away together to a world free of pain.

The man in the third armchair was talking in his sleep, his voice mingling with that of the radio announcer. He was restless. I covered him with a spare blanket and watched his wrinkled features for the fifth night.

In the last room along the corridor there was an unidentified patient who had been brought in burned and completely covered with bandages, without identity discs or papers. In a coma, he was dying and he was nameless. People were brought in to see him, to try to break the anonymity, to give him a past even if he had no future.

Four days the man in the armchair had been watching him patiently. Watching other people go in and out. His own son was missing, and something in the motionless heap of bandages told him to wait here for a sign.

The radio summed up the events of the day. "The morning was quiet on both fronts. Ground forces shot down three Syrian planes. The Egyptians tried unsuccessfully to advance in the north section of the canal front. Air force activities included the bombing of oil reservoirs in Syria and Egyptian airfields. The air force achieved complete air superiority in both fronts. The Iraqi force supporting the Syrians was defeated.

Tens of its tanks were destroyed and other units scattered and fled."

Were we listening? Somehow it was all too smooth. We had the upper hand in the air. The enemy was stopped short of the canal after crossing. The Syrians suffered heavy losses. Our forces were in control. There was something unbelievable in the reports. The patients told different stories. First of chaos and defeat, then of bitter unresolved battles. They spoke with awe of the mass of armor, of the powerful missiles. They talked of friends, dead or wounded.

Here at night the small size of the transistor seemed to minimize it all. The dry one-sentence announcements of the military spokesman were noncommittal, slightly vague and unnecessarily optimistic. Every day "our forces" repulsed enemy attacks. Every day "the enemy" suffered heavy losses. Every hour we were told of air superiority, but the helicopters kept landing, delivering bundles of pain who, when awake from anesthesia, told different versions.

"Are we winning again?" Shula asked. She wasn't being sarcastic, but her disbelief grew every time the news was announced.

"We are not losing. Maybe it's good for morale to smooth things, fog them for a while."

"In this fog there are people. Our sons and husbands and friends. I always believe truth is better, easier to take than disillusionment later."

Last night as we sat here, for the first time an announcement was made about casualties. After eight days of "our forces" and "enemy forces," there was a figure. Six hundred and fifty-six dead. All families had been notified.

Last night we sat in silence, counting in our hearts six hundred and fifty-six ungiven names, a long line of gravestones, the eyes of the families, weeping children, desperate mothers. Tonight we were back to the familiar war routine. The news as it was given and then the rest of the picture—rumors, personal reports, gossip, hearsay. During the day it all seemed real enough. The Egyptians crossed, there were bridges and surrounded strongholds. There were new defense lines and air battles and air support. There were the stories from wounded officers and doctors who flew in from the front. These were the unofficial experts, those who knew better than the others who merely suggested, analyzed, predicted, blamed.

But here at night, Shula and I, a professional and a volunteer, were at a loss. It all drifted into the abstract. The news of the missiles and the rockets and the artillery and the divisions, regular and reserve, were indigestible to us. The burns and the bandages were real, the red light above a door summoning a nurse was real. The helicopters landing with stretchers and limping soldiers, this was the war for us.

With the first light of winter dawn the ward began to live. The sedation was wearing off, and the first moans and murmurs were heard. I walked behind the nurse through the rooms. We gave thermometers, urine bottles, a wash basin to an early riser. Many were still asleep. I heard my name—"Amalia"—and turned to Uri, Rina's son. Amnon's son.

"I'm leaving today." He smiled.

"Good luck."

"I'll come and see you when I'm on my feet again."

"It will be over soon, there is talk of cease-fire."

"See you next war then."

"Very funny. You were not supposed to be in combat anyway."

"Sure. War orphans are exempted. I should have worked in the canteen selling chocolates, keep the quota down to one dead per family."

"Don't talk like that. Here, your mother is up."

She was standing there watching. A handsome woman with a restless smile. Still jealous of me for being loved briefly by a man dead six years ago, unable to bear the thought that I shared her memories of him. I spoiled the completeness of her widowhood.

Along the corridor in a small room, attached to a variety of tubes, was Lea's husband, Major Ilan, his chest and abdomen burned, his face unscarred. She was now standing near the window watching the wet grass covered with fall leaves. A handsome, strong man and a fragile, frightened woman counting time.

"He'll pull through," I spoke to her.

"I haven't heard it from the doctor."

"They don't promise. They don't like to."

"I knew it would happen. I knew it when he left the house on Yom Kippur." Lea's eyes were full of pain.

"He should have used the protective vest."

"They do at the beginning. The gloves, the head cover, then it grows hotter, it encumbers them and they take it off."

"He's seen burning tank crews before . . ."

She interrupted, "It would never happen to him, he used to say. They all feel that way."

"He is in the best of hands, you can get some rest."

"The nightmares are worse than the fatigue."

"I'll see you tonight. Take care."

She wanted to talk. I felt empty, unable to extend a hand. I never felt that way with the patients, but with the relatives I was at a loss. A guilt, the guilt of the untouched. My children were babies in bed, my husband was relatively safe. This was his fourth war and he was no longer in the front line. Here I was a volunteer in a white apron over a uniform, mechanically doing routine night duty. And feeling important about it. My insignificant life of mother and wife, of dishwashing and trips to the supermarket, suddenly gained another dimension.

I wasn't doing anything remarkable, I wasn't indispensable or irreplaceable, but I was there, a part of something major and horrible that was happening to us. Not the illusion of grandeur, no fantasies of being a lifesaver, but not a parasite either. There were people who fought and others who were defended by them, and I felt I belonged with the fighters, a drop of grease in a big machine, a square inch of blue in the painful gray sky. I glanced toward the unidentified soldier. The old man was in the room looking at him for the fifth day now.

Could it really happen? Could it be his son and still unrecognizable to him? Or was it wishful thinking? He knew the man was dying—why cling to the hopeless rather than go on searching? There were so many missing in battle, and every day more families were ushered in here. Most left with relief—no, it couldn't be their son, husband, brother. Yet he stood there, adopting what was under the sheets, hoping it was his.

The large room with twelve beds in it was lively

now. Smiling faces, jokes, the radio fully on, and the day nurse, fresh looking and energetic, pushing the breakfast cart around.

"The military spokesman announces that all night there has been an exchange of artillery fire in the central section of the canal front. The Syrian front was quiet and three terrorists were killed near the Lebanese frontier."

As the headlines were read everybody was quiet. A second later the chatter resumed. There were rumors of a planned crossing to the west bank of the canal. Somebody's cousin saw the large mobile bridges advancing yesterday.

"We'll give it to them from the rear. From Cairo and Ismailia it's the only way."

"You talk—I've been there. Right now it's their bridges and bridgeheads."

"Where do you think I came from? A fight in a nightclub?"

And so it went on, for those who were well enough to follow and argue.

It was time for me to drive home.

It was raining again, and I didn't feel too tired. The children were just up, pink-faced and vulnerable. Ofer was asking questions. Every morning he listened to the radio news and the information didn't satisfy him.

"There once was a war that lasted six days only," he said.

"This one is longer."

"How much longer?"

What could I say? "It will be over soon."

"Shall we go down to the shelter again?"

"I don't think so."

"Why isn't daddy fighting?"

"He fought in other wars. Now it's other people's turn."

"When will it be my turn?"

The little one was sure he was missing something. "And my turn?" he complained.

"One day there will be no wars, no soldiers, no missiles."

Ofer seemed to doubt the banal prediction, but it was easy to change the subject as we'd been through this unsophisticated routine before. They were not upset or worried. Their life—other than my absence during nights—went on as before. To tell them more was unnecessary, to avoid queries was impossible, so I switched to Cinderella and we laughed at the ugly sisters and the wicked stepmother until they were ready to leave for kindergarten.

A hot bath did not wash away the hospital odors, but it did calm the nervous tension. Every day I would sleep for a few hours and enjoy the first moments of waking up, believing it all had never happened. Just a dream. Yom Kippur had been an ordinary day, the war had never started, the canal never been crossed and the nightmare that followed was just another cruel fantasy. For five minutes, half asleep, I would think of the last days as an imaginary invention of a dark side of the brain. The minutes of "it never happened" were never long. The phone would ring, the sound of an airplane, the sight of a uniform on the chair tossed me back to reality.

There were things to do. The front was many miles

away. The rest of the country led a regular life. Kids went to schools, shops were open, supplies were not short, people did their work. Between the front and the home there were threads like a spider's web. The flow of information, the transistor radios in baby cribs or on playground benches, the latest edition of the newspapers in everybody's hands. Nervous teen-agers too young to fight hummed the new war songs. No lists of casualties, but the tears of those who knew formed a long rope between the battlefront and home. The brisk tension in every casual remark, the guilt of those remaining behind, anxieties unsuccessfully wrapped by routine activities. You could almost forget for a minute. There was no sense of danger in the city, just the shared ignorance of what was happening a few hundred miles away, and for me, the hospital—a nightly white reminder that it was not over yet.

When I volunteered, my mother doubted I could be of much use, but nevertheless agreed to stay with the children. In the afternoon she would come straight from the library where she worked, because "life should go on, that's our strength." We had never been too close, nor estranged. She lived her life, refusing to retire or become too grandmotherly. Working in the library, she acquired the habit of classifying everything and everybody, and her mind was constructed like shelves with numbered volumes placed along them. I was grateful to her, helping with the children. She couldn't really refuse, and perhaps it filled her evenings with some meaning, too. I heard her say to a friend, "Amalia is working in the hospital, so of course I take care of the children." But then, most things she did with a sense of duty rather than joy and we accepted this.

My husband came home late. At times we'd meet for a few minutes, exchange an understanding look, and I'd be gone. Gone with the feeling that he was convinced I needed the hospital duty much more than the hospital needed me. We never thought it would last so long. At the beginning I worked only in the morning, but when he half-blamed me for neglecting the children, I took on night duty. He was too tired at night to mind my absence.

Ward L, like most wards in the central hospital, was a long independent building. A waiting room, a nurses' station facing a dining room and a kitchen, and one corridor with seven doors leading to rooms of various sizes. The last two rooms each had one bed, the others were larger. The doctors had two rooms for examining and resting. Facing the patients' rooms were several bathrooms. The building was an old one, repainted tens of times, too cold in winter even with heating, and stifling in the summer.

Attached to the ward was an annex with three small operation theaters. These were used for minor grafts and changing of dressings under anesthesia.

"Sterility" and "infection" were key words in the ward and an endless supply of fresh gowns, masks and cloth shoes piled up every day in each of the rooms. Nurses were assigned to rooms and stayed with the same patients. The Professor didn't believe much in the textbook routine and these regulations were often broken. "I can't prevent mothers and wives from entering," Rothman used to say, "or make them look through windows, and bacteria develops in the patients even if they are isolated." So however hard we tried, there were people coming and going, some being helpful, others a tremendous burden.

For major surgery, the patients had to be wheeled on stretchers to the central building. Food was carted in five times a day from the central kitchens, as were medicines, blood and infusions in plastic bags. Nurses, volunteers, visitors walked hurriedly on the narrow pavements between the wards.

I arrived early for night duty. A one-line announcement cheered up the ward. The spokesman reported that a special task force had been active for the last twenty-four hours in the rear of the Egyptian forces, west of the Suez Canal, destroying antiaircraft missile sites and artillery units.

It was the first good news since the war began, other than the routine "repulsed" and "contained" and "counterattacked." For a moment we were back with our old image. Inventive, courageous, unconventional. Some, a few of us, were in Africa, in the rear of the horrible armor battles, in the vicinity of major roads and cities, where it could really hurt and change the picture. For the first time I had a vague feeling that this nightmare might come to an end soon.

The day staff was still around, two patients in wheelchairs watched TV. The Professor joined us. I sliced a cake I had baked at home, and we drank some sweet tea. He seemed to be in a good mood.

"For three good reasons" he said. "Major Ilan is out of danger. Still a long way to go, but he will live. A small bag was brought over from the emergency ward. Apparently it belonged to the man in coma. It may help the relatives who try to identify him, though there is no name on it.

"And I had word from my son-in-law. He is OK, up in the Golan Heights."

This was the most I had heard him say since the war began. Now he enjoyed the almond cake, and left for the central surgery building where he spent his nights. The night nurse came in with the American doctor, a volunteer, a specialist in burns, a Jew of Polish origin with a practice in Manhattan, yet not entirely out of place here on night duty in Ward L.

"Call me Leib, the way they do in New York," he said to the soldiers when he arrived. They talked to him as "the American" anyway, and watched him patiently as he looked for words in the pocket dictionary he always carried.

I translated the Professor's remarks for him, and his face lit up when I told him about Major Ilan.

"A fine man," he said. "A hero. I don't pray anymore, but I prayed for him."

He knew the Professor had a daughter, but you couldn't tell by the Professor's behavior that his son-in-law was in battle. He never disclosed a personal anxiety. We knew he loved music and played the cello, drove badly, and liked sweets. The rest of his private world was unknown.

When I told Leib about the bag apparently belonging to the unidentified patient in room 7, he grasped my hand. He was excited, somehow nervous about it. "Let's go and see!"

I wasn't sure we had the right. The nurse was on the phone softly calming a relative. Others were watching TV. Cease-fire did seem near, but fighting

was still going on. In the big room a singer was
playing the guitar, and Leib and I walked to the end
of the corridor to room 7. The door was always open.
The patient was breathing, but very still. Eyes closed
and head bandaged, the rest of the bed was sheets.
Odors of medicines and urine hung heavily. I opened
the window to let in some fresh air of wet soil and
leaves. An army bag hung on the rail of the bed.
An unmarked regulation bag. Dr. Leibowitz opened
it. Two cans of sardines, a tube of plum jam, C rations.
Nothing personal. A pack of cigarettes, matches, small
change. Socks, underwear—all army issue—and a
book. I examined the book page by page. No dedication, no pencil marking, not new and obviously read.
Monsieur Teste by Paul Valéry, in Hebrew.

"A hell of a clue," I remarked. "How impersonal
can personal belongings be?"

"Still, it's something."

"What something? For him the socks and cigarettes
were very personal items. For us here? Every single
patient arrives in the emergency ward with a pack
of cigarettes and a pair of socks, if he has a bag
that is. Only the others have names, discs, numbers,
mothers, something. Alive or dead, they have something."

"The book maybe. Is it a popular book here? Does
every soldier carry Paul Valéry to battle?"

"No. They carry books though, poetry, thrillers, student's textbooks. We are no detectives, Doctor. Just
trying to save lives here. If someone comes, and if
this someone is very close to this person, and if he
knew his reading habits and a hundred other 'ifs,'
maybe it will be a clue. And maybe he borrowed the

book, maybe he found it, or carried it for a friend. I can give you more 'maybes,' what's the use."

I, too, was overexcited. Ever since this person occupied room 7, I was haunted by him. First superficially, a mystery. A change, something bizarre. Then troubled, almost panicky. I couldn't stand the thought of a dying man being nameless. Not here, not in this land and this war. It was slow and tough and unexpected, but we were a family, we were all touched somehow. Our reactions and fears and anguishes were all human, and we related personally. He was the exception. The fact that he could exist contradicted all we knew and believed.

I closed the window. We left the room to meet Lea in the corridor. She hugged me. She could cry now, and did.

"It's a long night," Leib said, "we talk later."

CHAPTER 2

It wasn't such a long night. I wrote a letter for one of the boys who couldn't use his hands, and thought of my own copy of Valéry's book. Amnon gave it to me, eight years back, and even then it was out of print. A thin volume of a philosophical story emphasizing the victory of reason over emotion. I should look for it, I thought, when I heard the sound of a helicopter approaching.

In spite of the regulation red badges assigned to those permitted to go to the emergency landing site, a fence and strict orders, everybody was on hand for each new load of casualties. Everybody—doctors and nurses and volunteers and visiting soldiers. Most of us were just trying to identify faces. Doctors who were not on duty there but had sons in the front were pretending to give a hand, trying to steal a glance at the list of arrivals.

In an old wooden building next to the landing site, there was an improvised emergency room. The stretchers were brought from the helicopter, sorted out and sent on to surgery or wards.

Two soldiers with minor injuries could walk. Their

uniforms were torn and bloodstained, but they were planning their escape already.

"I should have never agreed to fly out here, they could have treated me in the field hospital."

"We'll get a ride back with the next copter. Hey nurse—" one of them spoke to me.

"I'm not a nurse, just Amalia. You better go in, you are bleeding."

"This can wait. Just a scratch. Where is the nearest phone?"

I promised him that he could use the telephone in Ward L if he would see the doctor first. His shoulder was covered with a bloodstained bandage.

"How is the coffee in Ward L?" he smiled and walked in.

Four others were wheeled into the operating rooms, two were destined for our ward. I walked back to help prepare rooms.

The helicopter took off, sprinkling us with dirty puddles of water from the runway. By the time I reached the ward a second helicopter had landed, then a third.

"And they said the war was practically over," Shula, the night nurse, said. "You'd better start making beds."

Uri's bed was empty. He had left during the day and so had his mother. I put on fresh sheets, and hurt my fingers pulling the edges, tucking them in tightly, putting energy into it as if half the cure were in a carefully made bed. Making beds in the hospital always made me think of my children. The rubber sheet under the cotton one—my little boy still needed it. The flat pillow—my husband believed it was bad for the children's backs to get used to pillows. Another sheet, a blanket, sheet over blanket, an inviting triangular fold of the free corner . . . I washed the side cupboard, which was intended for personal belongings, working by the neon light streaming in from the corridor.

Shula was pushing a bed from the waiting room. "Major Ilan is going to have company, so is room 7," she sighed. "The next one will have to be in the corridor."

Lea was dozing in the chair in the small room. I touched her shoulder. She was immediately fully awake, helping me push her husband's bed near the window and to make the new bed.

I told her how making beds made me think of my children.

"You're lucky they are young. Perhaps it's the last war."

"They said so in '67, too."

Empty beds, all made up, make me nervous, restless. The first day of the war, when all civilians were dismissed and went home or to other hospitals, this was the way it was. Empty white beds. We prayed then they should remain so, then two days later the hospital started filling up, as if someone felt these clean sheets deserved occupants. Now they looked to me like coffins with shrouds saying, "Here we are, come and bury your pain in sterile conditions. Shula and Leib and Amalia will watch over you so you can suffer in company. They'll cry with you and laugh with you and wash you and feed you and wish with you that you were never here, and hold the hand of your wife or daughter or girlfriend or mother."

I made another bed in the last room, next to the

unidentified "No 7," as we referred to him, and surgery called to say that there were two stretchers— second degree burns—on the way. One had a leg amputated as well.

They were pushed in by school teen-agers and nursed and transferred to the beds. Anesthesized, they didn't mind the inconvenience of transfer. In the morning they would ask, where am I and for how long and where is the mobile telephone? In room 7 I switched on the light. The face on the pillow was a face I knew. It was my brother's.

Not my real brother. Someone I used to call "my brother" all through high school. He was asleep and seemingly unharmed. I didn't dare look under the sheet. One hand was bandaged but the face, though pale and drawn, was unscratched. I looked at the chart attached to the bed. There wasn't much on it yet.

Avraham Goldin. Male. Age 32. Temperature 37° Centigrade. Blood count—normal; so was the pulse. Tomorrow morning the chart would be filled out. Right now it was like an identity card with a slight medical touch.

I felt weak for a brief second. My knees trembled. Not a face on a stretcher, not a hand on the blanket, not another chart, another name, but the face, the hand, the name I knew. Amnon's face surfaced to my mind. Avraham Goldin. It said age 32, but he was a boy, a teen-ager in shorts, never a fighter. I could never think of him as a soldier. We were the same age and yet here I was, a woman, looking at a boy with a new feeling. Something had just sunk in, a realization of the human involvement. Nothing could really justify the fact that Avi Goldin was a casualty of war. With the others, I knew it. Here, for a moment, I felt it, with sadness and compassion.

The headlines, the broadcasts, the figures and the reports helped me keep out. The war was a mechanism, a power struggle. The helicopters brought in casualties but they were just candidates for beds I had to make meticulously. Here was Avi. He was a person I knew, my brother, my friend. The long finger of the war had touched me too. The last time I had seen him was graduation day.

"Brother's" nickname was Avi. Auburn hair, freckled face, spaced front teeth, a mocking grin.

We lived in the same Tel-Aviv suburb. Avi had a natural talent for mathematics and science and used to help us all with the final exams.

What does one remember when looking at a "second degree ten percent" burn case back from surgery, last seen fourteen years ago?

Secrets. We shared secrets. He told me about his first love, her kisses, the feeling of her breasts. He tried to flirt with me once but we decided it was wrong and remained brother and sister. He told me about his first cigarette; his father was a radiologist and showed him X rays of diseased lungs which scared him out of smoking a second one. We walked home together every day. He was the first in the class to introduce T. S. Eliot and Dylan Thomas to our lives. He thought Thomas Mann and Hesse were the greatest fiction writers and made me read them.

Fragments of memories. Long legs sticking out of the shortest shorts. He used to kiss his parents on the lips. He served in the army and went with his family to the states. He was studying physics. His father got a job in New York and for all purposes they had left the country for good. Another classmate mentioned him once—"An emigrant," he said, "very successful." There were two letters. One announcing his graduation, the other his marriage.

My brother Avi. A long way from New York and family. Leib was watching me.

"You are smiling," he said.

"Yes. The new patient in No. 7 is from your city. Used to be from mine."

"Shouldn't we call his parents?"

"Better wait and ask him. He is a stubborn, capricious man, used to be as a boy."

It was morning. Among the cases admitted during the night, two were Egyptians. A separate room was allotted to them, together with a Syrian flown in at the beginning of the war. A military policeman was more or less stationed at the entrance to their room. He felt superfluous and disappeared often to wheel stretchers or help in errands.

The old man who so wanted No. 7 to be his son was gone. His son never smoked, he said, never used army socks, the book wasn't his. He'd go on looking.

I drove home in time to tell Daniel about Avi. I mentioned the Paul Valéry book, the Egyptians, Uri's transfer. He didn't seem to be listening. My life, my world, now, seemed like little episodes of no importance to him.

"Two, three days and it'll be over," he sighed.

"Not in the hospital."

"At least we are fighting west of the canal. Sharon did it again. I wish they'd let him earlier."

"The radio said 'a small task force.' Is it serious? Are they to be joined by others?"

"How do I know? I hope so. We stand a chance to win, and soon, if we fight from the rear. If we appear where they don't expect us, if we blow up the missiles and make air support effective."

Daniel didn't talk strategy to me, and even now he was having a dialogue with himself. Our eyes didn't meet, as if we all shared a shame. At weddings and Bar Mitzvahs we look people in the eye. At funerals we all look to the sky in protest or at the earth in agony.

The children were all around and busy. I touched them carefully, the way I did every morning as if I were contagious. As if I had no right to enjoy their softness until I was back with them.

My mother woke me; Dr. Leib was on the phone. He had talked to Avi, who said not to call his family. They didn't know he was in Israel. He was in Europe on vacation as far as they were concerned. Should we, nevertheless?—Dr. Leib wondered.

"He is not in danger, his life, I mean."

"No. Just, I think, if it were my son, I would have liked to be here."

"We'll talk to him tonight."

"I mentioned you to him. He said it was worthwhile being injured to have a reunion with you!"

He hung up. I wondered when he got to sleep, he seemed to always be around the ward.

My mother remembered Avi well. Rather as a "boyfriend" than a brother. My father was still alive when we were friends, and his admiration of anybody who could find science and math fun and easy found a good candidate in Avi. "He'll be somebody," my father used to say.

Mother thought we should spare the family the news until he got better and could talk to them himself.

It was Friday night. Before leaving I lit the candles with the children. Daniel said he'd come to the hospital later, if he could. My next-door neighbor brought in a cake for me to take to the hospital. Her face was drawn. She hadn't heard from her husband for a few days. His unit was across the canal.

"They don't have public phones there, you know. And no news is rather good news these days."

She was a cheerful type, always knitting and baking and trying new recipes for marmalades and jams.

"You are lucky to have something to do at night, something useful. Still, another few days and we'll throw a cease-fire party."

Fighting tears, she managed a clownish smile.

Friday candles were lit in the ward's dining room. I could hear a guitar and a woman's soft singing voice from the big room.

There were cakes and sweets and fruit on all the side tables. In the large room the regulations on sterility were less strict. Visitors were allowed and entertainment, too. The singer was a woman in her thirties, well known as a composer and performer. In 1967 we had met in the front line, just after the war. We were at the end of a battle and she had come to sing with a theatrical group. The woman has changed,

and so have her songs. A dimension of sadness replaced her joviality. The soldiers watched the ceiling
rather than her. Each one had his world of thoughts
or memories or wishes, and her voice caressed them
like an ancient prayer. It started raining and she was
crying. Singing and crying. There was no applause.
Someone asked for a song he wanted to hear, a Friday
night song from the Song of Songs. I walked past them
to room 7.

As if he knew my footsteps, before I fully entered
the room the freckled smile was all mine.

"Well, well, Sister. Just the way I imagined our
next meeting when we said good-bye."

"Very funny. Good to see you awake. How do you
feel?"

"You really want to know? Terrible."

"The pain will get less daily. Doctor Leib says you
are in good shape. Considering."

"Come on, who cares for the pain or the shape. It's
the location. I didn't travel this far to enjoy the medical services of Dr. Leibowitz."

"You did your bit."

"Sure. I even crossed into Africa. Got it on the
other side, at least not while defending but during an
attack. We are winning this war, if you didn't know."

I took the cake out.

"Should I call you Mother instead of Sister?"

As teen-agers we had been trapped in a teasing
game. Each had to be wittier, more cynical—intel-
lectual oneupmanship.

I felt as if this were a moment of truce. We were
two adults with lives behind us. One injured in a war
that was only partly his, I thought. Me, a mother of

two making beds for other mothers' big children. We can afford fatigue and seriousness. I told him so.

"Why don't you want me to call your parents?"

"Sure. This is Ward L. Central hospital. We have someone half burnt. New arrival from Africa. Claims to be your son." He changed his voice a little. "It must be a mistake, my mother would say. He is not in Africa, but in Europe."

"We said we were serious now."

"OK, serious. I'll fill you in. Graduation, remember? The army service, artillery officer. My father got a good job in a hospital and a scholarship for me. It was always for 'another year,' for another credit, a bigger savings account. Temptation was great. I was offered physics. I truly thought I'd be better equipped to contribute here when I returned. More excuses? My mother was not well, she is not well now. As a matter of fact, she has a couple of years to live." He paused, then, "How are your parents?"

"My father died in 1960. Mother is fine, working, busy. She sends her love."

"So I met this girl. From Springfield, Massachusetts. You've never heard of the place. A summer holiday love and a long winter of a bad marriage. One daughter. Separation. I decided to return—even if you don't believe me—and then my mother was hospitalized. My father was semiretired and aged suddenly. A story full of holes. We would all be better here—the sick, the aged, myself. But it would mean seeing my daughter very seldom. My mother recovered, became a great TV fan, father grumbles. I live on my own and 'dedicate my life to science.'"

The sarcasm I remembered was still there.

"The cake is great," he said.

He was exhausted. He shouldn't have talked so much.

CHAPTER 3

We sat in silence for a while, half listening to the singer. Avi asked whether she could come in. Dr. Leib joined us and so did the singer in a fresh white gown. She whispered nervously, "Should I sing here, with this guy asleep," pointing to No. 7.

"If you can wake him up you'll get a medical prize," Leib said somewhat bitterly.

Avi asked for a song which was popular two decades ago. The singer wasn't sure about the words and Avi sang along with her in a hesitant voice.

"And what's the most recent hit?" he asked.

She sang, "Let it be, let it be, oh please let it be. All we were to wish, let it be . . ."

"What's your wish?" Leib suddenly addressed the singer.

There were tears in her eyes again. An emotional woman trying to be strong. She stopped playing the guitar and looked at No. 7, hypnotized, then excused herself and hurriedly left the room. I followed her to the bathroom where she was sick and could hear Avi snapping unkindly, "That was some cheering up!"

Someone came in to say another ward was expecting her. She packed her guitar. I wondered how much more she could take, but she blew us all a kiss in the air and managed a smile and a confident, "Speedy recovery."

Back in the last room Avi tried to sit up.

"Now tell me about my roommate," he ordered.

"We don't know," I started. "He hasn't been identified. We have an estimated age—about thirty-five, medium height, fair hair, no fingerprints, teeth structure. The rest is either burnt or just unknown, a third degree case, full-thickness burns, no pain as nerve edges are burnt, too. Loss of fluid, kidney malfunction —the lot."

"I don't believe it," Avi stated.

"You see," Leib helped me, "he was brought in from a field hospital in Sinai, the third night of the war. He was stripped and bandaged and there were no discs. The battle involved several units, and there were many casualties and no accurate records. He was taken to Beer-Sheba, and then flown here. The unit responsible for identification and 'missing in battle' information has not come up with anything. There are no lists of casualties yet, and it will take a while before the computers are put to work on cases like this."

"Very cheerful company. It could be anybody, then. Someone I know, maybe, someone like me who is not supposed to be here in the first place—an Egyptian soldier perhaps. I hate the thought."

"So do we," I said. "There is also a bag, socks, cigarettes, a book by Paul Valéry, people coming in and out."

"Is he dying?"

The question, in an unexpected shrill voice, was

obviously addressed to Dr. Leibowitz. He didn't seem to react.

"Is he dying?" Avi repeated louder.

"It seems so. The fact that he is in coma means he can't cooperate. Medicine also needs willpower and the desire of the patient to struggle. It's the burns, and now the kidneys. The Professor sees in him some personal challenge, he nurses him in surgery as if he knew him." Reflectively he added, "He, too, can't accept the anonymity."

Avi was falling asleep. He had taken his "good-night" pill, as we called it, a while ago, and couldn't keep his eyes open.

We left for the doctor's room to warm up some coffee.

"Why does No. 7 bother me so much?" Leib half-asked, half-stated.

"It's inhuman, that's why, I suppose."

"Because it is happening here. I imagine a mathematical solution—all the casualties will be listed soon, those with names. Corpses identified and buried. By elimination of the known there will be, say, a hundred unidentified, or less. Then the computers will spill out names of the unaccounted for. There will still be some left, maybe No. 7 too. Maybe he'll remain till the last. If he is the only nameless one, that will be the final clue and someone will be sure to come for him."

"Not a very satisfactory process."

"It bothers me because we are a family. It's not a coincidence that you meet a relative here, a classmate there, someone who lives up the street or down the road or a block away. You are bound to, because you are a few and within a few circles—circles that cross and meet. You know each other. He pushes me back to the Nazi era."

Leib pulled back his white doctor's gown and the sleeve of his checked shirt to show me a tattooed number.

"I'm not being dramatic," he apologized. "We had numbers. Better than discs—only with burns deep enough the number is removed too. We were nameless but not anonymous. Somehow, when it is over and time to go home, I doubt that I can leave without making sure that this patient—alive or dead—has a name, an identity, someone who will place flowers for him in a vase or on a tombstone."

I must have fallen asleep, for when Shula gently touched my head it was dawn.

On nights like this I felt useless. Tired, unhappy, uninspired. An in-between person. Not young enough to spread youthful vitality around, not old enough to contribute motherly wisdom. Not pretty in a staggering way which could be a pleasure to some, but an ordinary face with regular features, decent figure and mild temper. I wasn't a professional but a fast learner, yet afraid to make a mistake and therefore not entirely independent. I fit into the job with a sense of duty, very little satisfaction and a nostalgia for other wars when it was all different.

Before going home I stopped at the rehabilitation center. I saw Uri briefly, brought him some sweets and magazines and was happy to see he was doing well.

"We should talk sometime," his mother said. "About old times."

"What is there to say?"

It was a bleak Saturday morning. I drove badly and impatiently for no reason. My mother must have noticed my mood for she offered to take the children to visit her sister. Daniel was asleep on top of the bed, still dressed. We were now alone in the apartment. It made me feel uncomfortable. Ever since the war started, I couldn't stand being touched, didn't want to make love. I rejected all affection.

I took it for granted that he understood.

Daniel wasn't really asleep. He watched me undress and get into the shower. He made room for me and though I planned to sleep in the children's room, I couldn't hurt him.

I lay there restless and irritated. Daniel sensed it.

"We are attacking now on all fronts. Syria, west and east of Suez."

"You sound like the military spokesman."

"I'm saying it to tell you it's nearing an end, not trying to boost your morale."

"I am exhausted."

"Why don't you ever cry? You used to."

He was a wise man. I loved him. I reached for his hand, saying to myself—don't be a fool. That's all you have and it's a hell of a lot. I missed the children and was sorry my mother took them away.

"Anything happened?" he asked.

"The same everything. Every day the same becomes less bearable. Repetition makes it no better—like playing on one string and reaching a breaking point."

"Would you rather work days again?"

How wise of him not to suggest I quit. I almost expected the "Haven't you done enough?"

"Perhaps. I'll talk to the head nurse on Sunday."

"Sleep now. I'll make some lunch when you get up. I have to be off in the afternoon."

You used to cry, he had said. There were no tears now, not for years, not as a handy weapon, not as an expression of self-pity, not as indulgence or release. Not much laughter either, the carefree rolling uncontrolled laughter was buried somewhere with the tears in the dull comfortable rather satisfactory routine. Long silences replaced the tears and a warm occasional smile substituted for laughter. Some kind of maturity, I supposed, settling for it.

Toward the evening we all went to the hospital. My husband visited a wounded colonel in the orthopedic ward and I took the children to Ward L. They had been there before. Ofer was fascinated by everything medical and behaved like a visiting professor. Rani dragged along. This was our, their life, and there was no way or reason to spare them. Children were part of the patients' life, too, and they enjoyed the children's visits, shared the heaps of sweets showered on them and told war stories from the fascinating never-ending "book of battles."

I had never taken them to room 7, for many good reasons. The ward's routine was hard enough to take without introducing the irregular. Now we went in because of Avi. The boys brought him drawings and we all pretended the other soldier was asleep. Avi told them how inadequate I was in school, and the children left a painting for "the other guy when he wakes up."

Daniel came in, chatted some, and took the children home.

When they left, Avi asked for the public phone to be brought in. He dialed 18 and asked the operator for a New York number, collect. I left the room.

In the waiting room I saw two familiar faces.

"Remember us, nurse Amalia? You promised coffee two nights ago!"

They were now in hospital pajamas but each had his army bag on the shoulder.

We went into the empty kitchen. In a cupboard there was some good Turkish coffee for special occasions, and we watched it boil, enjoying the smell.

"So you did stay, after all."

"We came to say good-bye. We are moving back tonight. We didn't have a chance to say good-bye to the nurse in Ward F. Please tell her in the morning we thank her."

It looked suspicious, pajamas and all.

"Do you have stamped passes?"

"Did anyone say the war was over?" They laughed They seemed well enough, but obviously they were running away and I was forced to be their partner.

They went into the bathroom and changed into uniforms brought to them by friends. The bandages were hardly noticed now, and they dumped the hospital stuff in the laundry room.

"It was a good forty-eight-hour vacation, and good coffee, but we won't be back here."

"My friend," the one said, "doesn't like the smells here, it makes him dizzy."

They were off before I could deliver a lecture on regulations and rules. I never asked for their names and presumed the nurse in Ward F would know and report properly. By then they would be wherever they wanted to be.

The supper cart arrived; I pushed it along the rooms. In the big room some Hassidic rabbis organized a prayer and song session, stopping only for the TV news.

It was the third Saturday of the war. How the tone had changed. The soldiers were watching the broadcast as if it were a bullfight. They were aware of the cost, but the announcements were confident and clear. The fog and vagueness were gone and it was obvious we were winning. The occupied area west of the canal was widened. Forces streamed in and enemy tanks, missiles, artillery were destroyed. The planes were shot down today and our advancing troops had full air support. The Syrian front was quiet.

The news carried me back to the Six Day War. The same expression of self-confidence and faith in the faces listening to battle reports.

I collected empty trays, returned the cart to the kitchen and walked to the end of the corridor. The last room was dark. I didn't switch on the light, presuming Avi to be asleep.

"Amalia? I am not asleep."

"Want some tea and cake?"

"Not really. I talked to my parents. To my wife and child."

"And?" I turned on a small light.

"I played the hero, I didn't have to, but I did. I could say I was here, alive and well and doing something or other."

"And you said you were in battle, wounded and in the hospital."

"Right. In a glorified way, as if insisting on giving them a guilt feeling, or anxiety, or a source of pride. And they are coming over as soon as they can . . . all four of them. I can't stand the idea. We'll have to think of something to stop them."

"They love you."

"Sure they do. Love doesn't have to express itself in presence. They'll come with my favorite sweets and the latest book and good American shaving cream and flame-retardant pajamas and the big wholesome feeling will become small change."

"Put yourself in their place. What other choice do they have?"

"What I did is put myself in my roommate's parents' place. That's what made me call. Suddenly I thought he'd better die and this scared me stiff."

In the door we could see one of the Hassidic visitors. He had a beard and side-curls and a black coat. His tallith was spotless white and he smiled broadly.

"So God is here, too," Avi said to him cynically.

"How do you feel today?" the man asked, in the softest of voices.

Avi relaxed. I left the room and when I looked in an hour later the man was still there and they were talking. Later Avi said they discussed the man in the other bed.

"The Rabbi said it's impossible. In a Jewish country there cannot be an 'unknown soldier.' 'We are a family, he said. 'We don't have recluses, hermits, not even priests. We are responsible for one another, we are a part of a pattern, with things in common and a common destiny.' No one is a 'nobody,' or even an 'anybody.' 'In a few days,' he said, 'his identity will be known. Someone will visit, his absence will be felt by somebody who cares.' "

"Let's hope so. In a couple of days you can move into the big room anyway. Two of the boys are leaving for rehabilitation, and you can have less disturbing company."

"You know I'll be disturbed by him wherever I am."

Major Ilan wheeled himself in, Lea following. He had a few maps in his lap and was making the rounds explaining strategy to whomever would listen.

He spread the maps on Avi's bed. "Your feet are north," he said. Avi's left hand held the Suez Canal and the East of Egypt section, on his waist lay the center—Tel-Aviv and the hospital area—and the beach ran along the left side of his body.

Ilan pushed the wheelchair toward the north. "Here, that's still left, Mount Hermon. We have to get to the top before cease-fire and hold control of the path all the way up. Only a very well-trained brave unit can do that, and you know which one I mean." He winked.

As if there were no time to lose in the midst of battle he turned along the bed and the map of Sinai. "Another unfinished story is the city of Cairo and the Ismailia-Suez road. This way we'll isolate the 3rd Army, destroy all missile sites along the bitter lakes and perhaps cut off the 2nd Army from Cairo as well."

"Don't point so hard, it hurts," Avi yelled.

"Sorry, my friend. I get carried away. I can't stand to be away from my unit."

Ilan's face expressed the excitement of planning.

His eyes reflected the sadness of someone who counts the casualties at the same time.

"In three days it can be done, if your people in Washington will only let us."

"His people are along the canal, just the way yours are," Lea said.

"OK, I take it back. Sensitivities again."

It all sounded easy in the sheltered room, on the map. I wondered how many helicopter landings we would have for each battle, how many more we could afford. Suez wasn't Jerusalem, I thought, but Ilan knows better.

"Nothing new here?" Ilan asked about No. 7 while leaving the room. Nobody bothered to answer.

CHAPTER 4

Rina was in the waiting room and we greeted each other politely. She said Uri was better now, and able to leave the hospital.

"Maybe we'll never meet again," she stated.

"Shalom, then. And good luck."

"I came here to tell you something."

"You don't have to." I didn't think that she felt like talking. I certainly didn't.

"I found letters. Your letters to Amnon. I should have given them to you, but I destroyed the lot. I feel badly about it, I had no right to."

"It doesn't matter. I can understand."

"It didn't help. The letters are gone, but you were there. Part of our lives, part of my memory of him. I was jealous and bitter, and then I realized I am thinking as if he were still alive."

"If he were alive, it wouldn't have gone on anyway. He never thought of leaving you, or the children. Why bring it all back now?"

"Was I not a good wife to him?"

"Too good maybe. The fact that a man has a good wife does not mean he doesn't have affairs. It just means more guilt."

"You weren't married then."

"No. I met Daniel after Amnon's death. As a matter of unhappy fact, on the day he was killed."

"Do you have letters from Amnon?"

"No. I didn't keep any. Didn't want to embarrass anybody." That was a lie. In the bottom of a drawer there was a thick envelope with letters written in Amnon's neat handwriting.

"Cone and see us sometime. Uri adores you. You've been good to him, and I was sulky and hostile. I really came to apologize."

"I might have behaved the same way in your place. It doesn't really matter, does it? What's important is that Uri is well, completely well."

We were all so kind, I thought. Forgiving and reconciling, full of grace and placability. A bunch of angels, all bitches and bad guys gone with the first round of ammunition. Our horrid beautiful war smoothed all wrinkles and differences and feuds. How shall we ever resume the normal balance again?

Another cease-fire, I thought when she left. A lonely woman living in a past she is forced to share.

With me. That way I shared a present with Amnon. Always a present. We never referred to past meetings, never remembered together things we did or said. We never planned the next meeting or thought together of things we might do some other time. We just loved, there and then and without a pattern that depends on continuity.

It was all romance, cornfields in full moon and deserted beaches on windy winter nights. And it was a rich man's romance.

Amnon belonged to a wealthy industrialist family.

They owned a chocolate factory, and he studied business administration at the best schools and joined the business. He was a cynic, but not without humor, and he was spoiled without lacking compassion.

I met him in a cafe on Diezengoff Street. I had a job with a publisher as a reader, a one-room apartment and lots of dreams. Vaguely I had a boyfriend, which means I had someone to go to the movies with once a week, but I wasn't in love. Amnon found an excuse to join my table. He said he was bored, married, rich, tired and also lonely.

No, he didn't want to go home because he didn't feel emotionally presentable to his wife.

"I shall enjoy the worst in you."

"Quite so."

First he showed off. He drove a big American car, so conspicuous I looked around to see if anybody had seen me get into it. He had a gold chain attached to a gold watch and smoked a Dunhill pipe. "Only the best," he kept saying, always adding, "and who needs it."

One hour after we met we made love and an hour later we felt we were in love. No life stories exchanged, no phone numbers, no preliminaries, just a head-on dive into a deep togetherness.

I must have smiled sitting there in the nurse's station, for Leib asked me what was funny.

"Pleasant memories. A man I knew who was killed in the Six Day War. Uri's father."

"Big love?"

"Yes. A man who had everything. I was part of this everything."

"Enjoy remembering," he said. "Right now past is better than present."

Money helps romance. There were flowers instead of phone calls, messages delivered by hand, carefully chosen little gifts and, naturally, lots of chocolates. Amnon was of medium height, on the short side. He wasn't active in any sport, but he had a wiry body and a sportive look. Expensive clothes but no tie, seldom a suit, canvas shoes.

After a couple of weeks of brief happy meetings an envelope arrived. A ticket to Eilat and a note attached—"Meet me at the Red Sea Hotel, room 15 tomorrow night."

I was not a "woman of the world," I wasn't carefree in my actions, not even a very daring or adventurous person, and here I was, telling a lie to my mother and boss, packing an overnight bag with a flimsy nightgown and a bathing suit, wearing dark glasses and a straw hat, and flying to Eilat without even feeling ridiculous, just silly and happy.

In my happy-memories drawer, the day in Eilat is a gem. No clouds, not one moment of moodiness or regret, not even an artificial "Let's have fun and if we don't let's pretend." Was it the lovemaking? The fact we both loved desert air and freedom, our lack of need for words though we talked a great deal? Mostly it was the joy of not constructing something for future references or memories but only for that same moment's fun. We walked, we ran along the beach, we swam at night, we ate grilled fish, and the next day we took different flights to Tel-Aviv without the obvious "When shall I see you again?"

And again and again.

Loving Amnon was not a full-time job. I didn't sit there waiting, I didn't worry or think about things he might be doing when he wasn't with me. We didn't lay bricks in order to build something. Each meeting was a colorful transparent bubble.

He seldom mentioned Rina; when he did it was with affection and respect. His heart could accommodate us both easily.

A careless playboy in his social life, Amnon was very prompt and responsible whenever work or reserve-service was concerned. Business was no pleasure, but it was exciting and challenging. Though he hated chocolates or sweets, he had a sense for marketing and advertising, and he enjoyed expanding, taking risks, introducing new products and keeping a strict eye on quality. Army service every year for thirty or forty days was sacred. Once in uniform, he became almost a different person—serious, concerned, all cynicism gone. When he spoke of "my regiment," it was with profound caring. No nostalgia for youth, just suddenly a sense of responsibility taking over.

When he was in the service, we saw each other a great deal. He'd come for an hour very late at night; he wasn't expected at home, and his regiment was stationed an hour's drive away. The uniform looked right on him. The gold chain was gone and a stainless steel watch replaced the gold one. He made love as if he were facing a battle the following morning, and then talked of "his men, his tanks, his guns, his officers," with a sense of possession. Not monopolizing, just owning gently.

He was a pessimist. He saw disasters around the corner and talked a lot about the next war.

"Not that we won't win it, but there will be losses." He used to say he knew who would die in the next war. "Sometimes I look at my men, and I know the doomed ones. I almost feel like getting them a transfer, as if my premonition is going to contribute to their death."

"What about you?" I tried to be lighthearted about it. Surely he wasn't a candidate.

"No. I'll be all right. Not immune, but they won't get me. I'm beyond, in age and rank, the stage of being burnt alive in a shelled tank. It used to terrify me in '56."

And here I am, I thought, in Ward L, filled with armor casualties caught in burning tanks. How different my life would have been were Amnon still around! Then faces, as in a movie, in a series of associations passed through my head. Rina, the Rabbi at the funeral, Uri as a boy, as a soldier, Daniel, my own children, my wedding, my own fearful face in the desert when I heard of Amnon's death. Then back to Ward L and Avi, Leib and finally No. 7, faceless, nameless. Always back to No. 7, as if he signified something important for all of us.

Morning light invaded my memories when the public phone rang. The overseas operator had a person-to-person call for Avi. I plugged the phone in room 7. Avi was asleep and I tried to wake him gently. He jerked up, which hurt him, cursed and swore again when he saw my frightened expression.

"I'm sorry. A call from the States."

"Hell. Don't they know of time difference? What time is it?"

"Five the next day. Talk and go back to sleep."
I gave him the receiver and left the room.

"You don't have to be so well-mannered. You can
listen in. No secrets, Sister."

It was his wife. They were all coming over. The
minute they could get on a flight. Does he need anything, do the hotels function, is it safe to bring the
child, what's the weather like?

He was amused and furious. One minute it's a
family mourning over a wounded son, the next day
he is a travel agent running a postwar tourist
attraction.

"Come and see Israel licking its wounds. Reductions
in the Hilton shelter for parents of injured and dead.
Half price on air tickets for those in time for a
funeral."

"Stop it. It's good that they are concerned with
the minor things, kind of self-defense. Your father
can take over for one of the overworked radiologists.
Anyway, you'll be happy to see your daughter."

"Sure. Straight from Springfield, ponytail and Bugs
Bunny. A nice introduction to a country I described
as one long white beach with seashells and water-
melon stands. All my neurotic wife needs is the
storyless story of my roommate."

"We all cope with it somehow."

"Do we? We push it aside and keep thinking.
Remember T. S. Eliot's 'The Hollow Men'—that's
what I keep reciting when I look at him. Please get
me out of this room."

I waited for the day nurse. The Professor came in
first and, as he always did, went straight to room
7. There he stood looking at his mystery patient,

every morning expecting the miracle which didn't happen.

Avi mentioned to him the possibility of a transfer. "In a couple of days, I think. It's quieter here, good for you."

"Sure it's quiet. What it doesn't do to my eardrums, it does to my nerves. My family may show up. I'd rather see them surrounded by all those handsome noisy burnt heroes in the big room."

"You can take Major Ilan's bed, he is leaving soon. Only there, his roommate is an amputee, and phantom pains are not good company either."

"Any good news this morning?"

"Still talk of a cease-fire, in a couple of days or so. Last days' battles are the worst, though. Done in haste, a certain carelessness, as if fate's verdict is given already and there is no danger."

I spoke with the day nurse; she thought, if I could and didn't mind, that she could use me better during the night.

"Too many help during the day. We lose control. Mothers and wives of volunteers and teen-agers and missions of ladies bringing in transistor radios and chocolates and shaving cream. What we really need is a guard to keep them away. In your calm manner," she said, "you are a great help." Calm manner. Quiet way. This was me. Insignificant in the background. Unobtrusive manner of giving urine bottles, watching infusion containers without screaming in ecstasy, serving food without doing a belly dance. Reassuring, a good listener, a bore maybe.

Not with Amnon. Then I could be crazy, do things that normally would be only daydreams. Dress funny, talk funny, do the unexpected, argue, fight and then laugh and be free.

The day nurse touched my shoulder.

"Go to sleep, we need you fit tonight, it's not over yet. Not at all."

She too was a bore, so we got along well. Did she, too, have fantasies? Did she ever have an Amnon to be wild with? Hair in a bun, impeccable starched apron and cap, small soft hands, she didn't look it.

I drove into town to do some shopping for the children. Little toys, sweets, warm underwear, compensating for absence.

The shops were all open and the main street quite gay. Every woman in town seemed to be shopping nervously, holding a shopping bag or a baby or both. I sat in the cafe where I first met Amnon. The wooden chairs had been replaced by plastic ones and the coffee wasn't as good. I felt guilty, the way most civilians did. A sunny winter day in a pavement cafe. Somewhere there was a battle. Somewhere there were soldiers, sons and fathers of others, running, falling, shooting, advancing and retreating and reloading and advancing again. Somewhere there were other sounds, shells exploding, bombs falling, chains of tanks, communication sets, hoarse voices of exhausted commanders, jets diving. And it wasn't in the movie house, it was "our forces." And "our forces" were people we knew and the sounds and the sights didn't reach us and when we switched off the radio it was as if it had never happened. Here, in the city, there was a life free of bullets and shells, not even sirens. Just the expression in women's eyes, remembering and waiting, hoping and counting the lonely nights and long days and waiting.

"Anything else?" the old waiter asked.

I paid and stood up. I remembered him from years back. For him I was just another face, for me he was a reminder of my other life, as brief as it had been.

Next to the cafe, I walked into a bookstore. The owner knew me, for I came in quite often.

"Not much business?" I asked.

"On the contrary. Women buy, either to escape into reading or just for the sake of purchasing. How is the family?" Whenever anybody dared ask, they lowered their eyes. It was a risky question these days.

"Fine. My husband is not in combat, my brother was heard from a couple of days ago. I am stationed in the hospital." He asked me to see a relative in Ward B, if I happened to pass by, and asked me about the surgeon there.

"Do you have Paul Valéry's *Monsieur Teste?*"

He pondered. "No, it was a small edition, never reprinted."

I mumbled something about having bought it there with a friend ten years back.

"Must have been before '67," he said.

"See you soon."

I drove along the waterfront. Black clouds were gathering and I hoped to make it home before the heavy rain.

Whenever anyone talked about the next war, it was placed in summer or spring. "If there is no war next summer, we may go abroad," Daniel said every winter. So did Amnon. War in the winter or late fall was all wrong for both sides. Yet it was raining, roads became paths of sticky mud, visibility was lowest, nights were chilly and the war did go on. Only in the burns ward did they think winter war was preferable because fluid loss was lower. Women were knitting woolen caps and pullovers "for the front," truckloads of woolen socks were passed out and army kitchens were busy warming up soup.

When I got into bed it was raining, when I woke up the battle on the Hermon was on.

I remembered Ilan's map on Avi's body. Mt. Hermon and the city of Suez, two battles to go.

I got up and started cleaning the apartment. A battle was going on in the north, in narrow paths and up the cliffs, in the fog and wetness, and I had to do something to keep busy. I mopped the floors, did the hand laundry and cleaned the bathroom with fury and boredom and utter frustration. I could hear helicopters and planes going by, north or south, carrying ammunition or casualties. I could hear the baby next door crying, a loud voice of a neighbor on the phone, winter birds, seagulls and wagtails, leaves falling, my own tired footsteps behind the vacuum cleaner. And this was the war. The toughest of the wars, and my anxiety was only skin-deep. I wore the mask of a worried person. I didn't want people to die or be injured, but there was no earthquake deep inside. A wait, a vigil, time counted and measured mechanically. I wanted to care more, I wanted to cry. There were no tears, just a lot of work to do, and I carried on with shame and guilt until my mother came and the children arrived and it was time to return to the hospital.

I noticed at the gate an unusual commotion. Cars coming and going, ambulances, doctors and nurses gathering around the emergency ward.

"Just preparing," someone said. "The Hermon battle is still on and we won't know yet how many we'll get tonight."

Ward L was quiet. Room was made for more beds, three guys from the big room left and two more were transferred to the orthopedic ward. The staff was all there, day nurses stayed on and the Professor took a nap in his own room.

Major Ilan in a wheelchair was holding the map and talking on the phone. Others gathered around him, as he was a source of information.

"It started well," he said. "The paratroopers did a good job. It was a face-to-face, snipers and hand grenades battle. The infantry division is in now, trying to get another stronghold, and there it's bloody. It looks like it'll last the whole night."

"I wish cease-fire had started yesterday," Shula whispered.

"Without the Hermon?" Ilan jerked.

"Without more dead."

"Sure. Another defeatist. Another couple of years when the Syrians are there and shoot down at you from the white height of the moutain, you may regret every dumb pacifist thought you have now."

Lea tried to hush her husband.

"We are all nervous, that's all. It seemed almost over and now, emergency again, and casualties, and how much can people take."

"As much as necessary. Whatever we manage to

take before a cease-fire is a lifesaver in the future. We are not fighting to secure a ski resort."

The supper trolley arrived and interrupted a hopeless argument. When I arrived with the food in room 7 I thought I had entered the wrong place.

Avi lifted himself up with effort and pointed at No. 7. He was as still as before, not a wrinkle in the sheet, but in the evening silence we could clearly hear the vague sound of a man crying. And there were tears. The mouth didn't twitch, the body seemed dead but somewhere in this bundle of mystery the tear glands were operating and alive, and the liquid salty drops rolled down to be absorbed in white gauze from the cheekbones down.

"How long has he been crying?"

"Just a minute ago. I talked to him, having nothing to do, the way I do often when we are alone, and suddenly I felt his presence. He didn't say a word, but I sensed a difference. So I looked up and I saw the tears."

I left the room to call the Professor. He was asleep, but the minute I touched his shoulder he was wide awake.

"The unidentified. He seems to be crying, weeping that is."

The Professor's face brightened, without a smile. We walked to the room and stood above No. 7 and watched. The tears were still flowing, but not a sound or a motion.

"I talked to him," Avi said. "I asked for his name a hundred times but there is no reaction."

"Keep talking. You, too, Amalia, better stay here

a while and watch. Perhaps it's a beginning, a crack we can use and widen."

He must have seen similar tears before, for he was less hopeful than I thought. I mentioned it to Avi.

"Sure. He passes urine, too, perhaps it's a kind of reflex, or a drug that was injected into him. Did it ever occur to you he may be pulling our legs? Just quietly taking a leave from our petty preoccupations?"

"Back to cynical, are you? Any news from the family?"

"Any day, Sister, and if you are a real friend you'll get them on a six-day tour of battlefronts, a trip to liberated Africa or the holy Mount Hermon or whatever tourists will be shown after this war. How is your family?"

"All right. Runny noses, crying more than usual. I am not a very good homemaker these days."

"You've changed a great deal altogether. I didn't want to talk about it, but since you asked."

"I didn't ask anything."

"Still. It's not the fun girl we knew. A sparkle is missing. Either you are very bored, or very tired, or very hungry for something that isn't there. Drifting in and out of scenes without participating. Not aloof or remote, just absent."

"So, doctor, what's the cure, supposing the diagnosis is right?"

"An exciting job or a fantastic lover. The second is better."

"Thanks a lot. Very banal too. 'Find a lover and your problems will disappear.' Nonsense. I wish it were that easy."

We were talking to each other while looking at

No. 7 like an infusion bag emptying. The tears were shed at intervals now, then stopped.

I switched off the light. Avi needed sleep more than all my chatter, and I had to clean beds and prepare them.

I told the Professor that the crying spell was over. He merely nodded and I found myself saying, "I wish my tears were running these days."

"Many of us find it difficult to cry. The tension strangles the tears. Nurses feel inhuman because they don't cry, are not moved by all the pain and agony surrounding them."

I regretted ever mentioning it, apologized and smiled.

"I suppose it'll all burst out one day. When it's over. When we don't have to be strong superwomen."

"I just talked to the Rambam Hospital in Haifa. They are preparing rooms, and we may not need the extra beds here."

"Better to have them ready and not use them."

I called home. Daniel wasn't there. I woke my mother up. She was patient and understanding, her usual self. "No, Daniel didn't say whether he was coming in tonight." She had given the children cough syrup and they were sleeping well.

The boys didn't have a cough, but mother was a believer in preventive medicine. I apologized again and hung up. Then it crossed my mind that the same suggestion Avi had made to me might have occurred to Daniel. He had all the good reasons to have an affair. A wife who wouldn't be touched as long as the war was on, a mother-in-law who put things in order before you even used them, a job, important, but away from the front line. He must feel old, perhaps unwanted, and yet he is handsome, virile, thoughtful and attractive to women.

"He is not the type," I always said to myself. But not being the type makes him more vulnerable and available. He may even be in love.

With a girl like Amnon had, dashing, daring, careless, sensitive and entirely different from his wife. Maybe a married woman whose husband is fighting in the Hermon or stuck across the canal. He knew how to comfort loneliness.

The more I thought of it the more real it seemed. While cleaning the first bed it was an amusing supposition, stretching sheets on the second bed advanced it to a clear possibility, and while pushing the third bed into place I already had it clear in my mind. It was a reality. Daniel, my model husband, was having an affair with a vivacious blond. She had deep brown eyes with a naughty expression. She was fun in bed and they carried on while the war was on, while I was fighting the smells and sights of Ward L.

I finished working, satisfied with my new role as a victim, feeling slightly sorry for myself, somehow heroic. I wasn't just anybody, I was a betrayed woman.

CHAPTER 5

On the bedside table I found a note. From Daniel. In casual, well-spaced words it said that he was going south, to be of whatever use he could be in his division Headquarters in the Sinai. Especially now that the war was about to end, there would be a need for logistic experts. He would be in touch whenever possible. Kiss the children and thank my mother, signed "love." He didn't write his name at the end. What for? Who else could it be?

For a brief moment I carried on with my previous fantasy. He had a girl, he took off. He drove south perhaps, but not alone. I took a shower and relaxed. It was the obvious frustration, he needed to be involved, even if only at the end of the war. He had to be there. He was a man who fought well and often. Some of his friends were still in the front, and he couldn't stand this nervous civilian inactivity any longer. It seemed natural and I felt it was the right thing to do. Were I in his place I would have done the same. Maybe earlier.

It posed problems, of course. I hoped my mother would be cooperative, for it would mean more hours with the children, if I were to continue at the hospital. I didn't dare think of life without the hospital routine.

I knew the war would be over, the beds in Ward L would be occupied by sick civilians, the doctors would work regular hours and all the good volunteers would go home. I knew and welcomed the knowledge, but for me, Amalia, it was just a vague memory of what life before had been, rather than a desire to resume it afterward.

I looked into the cupboard. Daniel had taken his uniform with him—battle dress and heavy shoes, underwear. In the bathroom his shaving kit and tooth-brush were missing. It occurred to me we had never been apart since we had been married. We had never slept in a hotel bed or gone on a trip together. In six years there was not one day, for either of us, of not seeing the other. Now that he was gone—and not just for the day—he was still here. There was matter-of-factness in his absence, just as his presence had been taken for granted before. That's because we are friends, I thought.

I washed my hair and baked a cake and the children came home from school, lovely and sweet. I explained to Ofer about Daniel's departure. He seemed proud; he would have liked to have seen his father in uniform.

Ofer wanted to see a map. I pointed out to him the road along the beach, south, then west all the way across Sinai to the canal.

"The other side is Africa, Egypt. Your father may be there soon."

"Will he shoot anybody?"

"I doubt it. The war is over, you know."

"Will he come back?"

"Of course."

The child seemed pensive. There were many questions he didn't care to ask and I didn't encourage him. All my conversations with the children about war seemed trite and irrelevant. I didn't want them to hate, I didn't want them to take the state of war for granted. There should be a school for mothers, I thought, teaching us to handle children in wartime, which seemed to be all the time.

My mother was surprised and sarcastic. "A bit late in the battle, isn't it? Did you have a fight or something?"

We never fought, and she knew it well. It simply didn't fit her organized head. The unexpected never did.

By the late afternoon all the Hermon peaks were in our hands. Golani, the infantry division, had suffered heavy casualties, fifty dead and twice the number wounded. The cease-fire was set for the early evening. Only the city of Suez was not in our hands.

Before leaving work, I called a few friends and told them Daniel had gone south. I asked for some help with the children, and shared the relief of the cease-fire news.

I didn't really feel like leaving the apartment. The children must have noticed it and clung to me for attention and stories. They didn't eat well. Ofer was coughing, and my mother emerged with the famous syrup.

I felt guilty leaving them. Ofer refused his medicine and was crying. My mother seemed hopeless and old and tired and I felt she'd rather be elsewhere. Rani held my hand and wouldn't let go and then started crying, too.

I called the ward to say I'd be late and I sat with the boys in their room building a castle from wooden blocks.

Ofer relaxed, but he was absentminded, talking in incomplete sentences and his eyes filled with tears whenever I looked at him. Rani was aggressive. He enjoyed knocking down the towers we built and refused to gather the blocks. I thought of staying home, but Ofer said, "Why don't you go, Mother, it's late."

I held him for a long moment. He didn't return my smile or hug, just let me fondle him. We both knew he wasn't a baby anymore, and if I pretended he was, he kindly tolerated it.

What went on in their little heads? What went on in my mind when I was Ofer's age and my father was fighting in the War of Independence? I vaguely remember my mother explaining to me that we were going to have a state of our own. I remember crying when her brother, my uncle, whom I don't remember, was killed in that war. My father returned and we were together again and I was left with no scars or memories.

Rani fell asleep on the bed, fully dressed, and Ofer went into the kitchen where my mother, composed and seemingly relaxed, talked him into drinking hot milk with honey. I left quietly, wishing I could cope better, and took off along the wet familiar road to the hospital.

*　　*　　*

Looking at No. 7 I remembered Daniel had no
identity discs. But there was no worry, the fighting
was really over. He would sit and chat with his
friends, they would plan the supply lines and the
release of reservists, they would argue the political
scene late into desert nights, communicate with Headquarters for instructions and criticize them, suggest
how things should have been done and weren't, eat
the rations and dream of home-cooked meals and
eventually return home.

There were a lot of people in room 7. They were
talking in English. The cheerful loud voices of Avi's
family. The nurse told me he was being transferred to
another room, replacing Major Ilan who had left. The
amputee there was feeling better and the big room
was full again with transfers from other hospitals. The
family had been told No. 7 was asleep, and with the
excitement of reunion, he was ignored.

I looked at them for a while before entering. The
parents had aged and changed. Avi's mother, a plain,
round-faced, plump woman as I remembered her,
was now a slimmer, tougher-looking American lady.
Every movement of her hand produced the rattle of
half a dozen bracelets with charms and her hair was
an unidentifiable color, between mauve and gray.

His father simply looked bolder and older, and was
criticizing the "hospital conditions," referring to the
fact that his son, who came all the way from Manhattan to the canal, could be placed in a better-heated
single room.

Avi's wife, Julie, was pretty. Fair hair, childish expression of surprise and astonishment and a skinny
figure in jeans and a cashmere sweater. The diamond

ring and small earrings were just a warning not to be misled by the jeans, a modest announcement of hidden, carefully used affluence.

The little girl, Karen, resembled her mother, but had Avi's curly red hair, and was busy listening and trying to fight sleep.

I was introduced, and embraced and kissed by the parents while asking them to wait in the waiting room. Shula and I pushed the bed to the vacant place, and Avi looked for my hand at the side of the bed.

"Don't leave me now," he said. "I am glad they are here, but please stay around."

He asked Shula to tell the doctor his family had arrived, and to ask if the doctor would explain to them that he needed rest, that they should come during visiting hours only.

"They'll see that everybody else is around."

"Just tell them so. They are an obedient lot. Leib can do it for me."

They all returned, intensely practical. They arranged the side-table with little gifts of marshmallows and shaving lotion, transistor radio (the third Avi got in a week) and mouthwash. A drawing made by Karen, who was asleep now, was pinned to the wall. Chairs were brought in and arranged in a circle.

Avi's new roommate was curiously watching the scene. He had a bandage covering his nose and ears but his black eyes were shining. He didn't understand the language, but it was a change and he was amused. Avi's mother addressed him. "We speak Hebrew, except for Julie." She went on to take inventory. No, he is not married, he is only nineteen. He is from a village in the Galilee, his parents can't come often because the turkeys have to be tended, he has five brothers and sisters, no, he doesn't need anything, no, he is not bashful and will say if he does.

"Well," she concluded, "you'll soon be on your feet, back to the farm."

"On one foot," he mumbled. He didn't care much about the leg, it was the damaged face that bothered him. What was left of his nose and ears could not be hidden forever by a white dressing.

Avi was embarrassed. He explained in English that the boy had lost a leg, that he had been outstandingly courageous in the fight for the Golan, and asked his mother to leave him alone.

"I love them all," his mother stated, with no apology.

I left them to the chatter and walked back to room 7. It was just as I had seen it at first. One bed in a darkened room with an aura of unspoiled whiteness. Avi gone, his living smells gone, too. The sounds had disappeared, and there were odors of medication, urine and disinfectants mixed with the silence of motionlessness.

Shula offered me some coffee, when Avi's skinny wife appeared at the door. She wanted to ask something.

"Please," she whispered, "I'd love to do some work while I am here."

I mentioned the imminent cease-fire, said there wasn't a need, suggested she should see the country, visit Avi, meet people.

She was stubborn. "I am not playing volunteer. I mean it. It doesn't have to be here, in this ward. It isn't even because of Avi. You know we are separated.

Karen can stay with her grandparents, but I have to do something, anything."

"Talk to Dr. Leibowitz about it," I suggested. "He may be able to think of something."

Leib woke up from an after-surgery nap and came in for coffee. He shook Julie's hand and behaved as if it were a Manhattan cocktail party. Offered her cake, a chair, a cigarette, obviously impressed with her clean, innocent, unbelonging looks. They talked about restaurants in Boston. The New York City Ballet, Martha's Vineyard. Their world. She seemed comfortable encouraging his nostalgia, and he was grateful to escape for a moment from his Hebrew pocket dictionary and medical preoccupations. He offered to take her around the hospital the next day, to help her find something to do.

After midnight they were all gone. Avi was asleep, but his roommate, Nadav, whispered my name.

"Are they very rich, his family?"

"No, why?"

"They've been in America for so long, I wondered. Was thinking about my parents, how tough their life is, how unexciting."

"What's so exciting about being in America?"

"I've never been. Why is Avi separated from his wife?"

"Who knows. It happens here, too, doesn't it?"

"She is so pretty. Christian, is she?"

"Yes. Go to sleep now."

"I want to go home." He whispered like a very small child.

"You will, soon."

"What will I look like when they remove the bandages?"

"It's a long process. You'll probably have plastic surgery. They'll reconstruct it all, handsome and new."

"I rather liked my old self. So did my girlfriend."

"I hope she loves you for more than your nose and ears."

"I have nightmares. I see my monster's face in them."

"Listen, now. There are cases worse than yours. They function perfectly well. Don't fall into self-pity."

"Sure. All the girls are waiting for the one-legged burnt-faced hero to come back home. On the farm I can be useful as a scarecrow."

"The army will help you study, if you care to."

There was silence. Julie's perfume was still in the air and if Nadav was weeping he did so without sound.

In the big room there was still commotion. Two soldiers were arguing about the battle of the city of Suez, about the face-to-face fighting and the types of hand grenades used. On one of the beds I saw a soldier's girlfriend, asleep. She was in uniform, exhausted, and I didn't have the heart to obey regulations and wake her up to leave.

Leib, in the nurses' station, was wide awake. His encounter with Julie transformed him momentarily into a silly youngster. The tragic weight of war coupled with Jewish self-pity was gone, replaced by mid-Manhattan affectations. He bored us with a few stories, attempting sophistication, and while Shula and I fell asleep, he carried on.

CHAPTER 6

"Have you ever been to Europe?" Shula asked me.

"Yes. Twice. Once on my own, another time with a friend. Why?"

"I am thinking of going. When this is all over, I'll leave the children with my in-laws and go."

"Well-deserved trip. Where will you go?"

"I don't know. Places one hears about, London, Paris, perhaps Venice and Florence. A regular tourist. That's what I'd like to be. Read the guidebooks, take tours, see things of beauty. I am entitled to a month's leave, and we have some savings."

"Great idea. Better wait for spring, though."

Europe in the spring was Europe with Amnon. Two months before he was killed.

He had to attend a conference in Geneva and we planned, he planned, to meet in Paris. He gave me the tickets, the name of the hotel, the date—the way he did when we met in Eilat. He even packed for me, throwing out of the suitcase half the things I thought I couldn't do without. He gave me some money and tokens for the Paris public phone in case I got stuck, and he left three days earlier for Geneva.

I didn't take this trip for granted. It wasn't less

moral than sleeping together in my apartment, but I did feel guilty. His wife could have gone if it weren't for me. She had on other occasions.

"That's why," he said. "Your turn now."

He never mentioned the expense involved and I didn't think of it, although alone I couldn't have afforded it. I told my mother and friends that I had saved enough for the trip, needed a change and a vacation. They never questioned it further and saw me off at the airport.

It was raining in Paris and gloomy when I arrived. The trees were just beginning to bud and it was cold. At the hotel I found Amnon hadn't checked in yet, and I went for a walk.

The pale sun broke through the clouds, changing the city from a slave to a bride with magic light. My rusty French won me a smile at the cafe, and walking back along the quay I felt as free as only a woman in love can.

Amnon was waiting with chocolates in a fancy box and fruit in brown paper bags. He unpacked both cases and placed everything neatly in drawers.

He told me about Geneva, looked at the Hebrew newspapers I had brought along, phoned room service for Evian and undressed me.

"First we make love. Then we go for a drive and some food, then we make love and go out again. What would you like to do?"

"Do I have to say? I missed you."

"Don't ever say that. Just enjoy what you have."

Enjoy I did. The week in Paris was a finishing school. I learned all the superfluous things a chic person should know. What to eat and where and how.

The little place on the Île St. Louis served the best ice cream (prunes and Grand Marnier), at Fauchon we got the best *tarte au citron* and on the Place Victor Hugo these fancy little sandwiches and tea in a glass. For a dressing gown we went to Porthault and at Charles Jordan he knew the salesgirls by name. I didn't care for shopping but after three days I felt natural in a Cacharel skirt and blouse, shoes and bag to match, a new trench coat, sunglasses, even a key chain and a wallet.

"So, only the poodle is missing," Amnon said.

We went to galleries and argued about paintings. He made me try all the seafood delicacies I had never believed were edible, and we danced at night until my feet were swollen in the new shoes. We made love in the hotel room and kissed at every street corner, and for the first time I thought about the future. Thought, not talked. I was spoiled now. I could never use plastic instead of leather, synthetic instead of fine cotton or silk, underwear without fine lace. Or at least I thought so.

"It's all nonsense of course," Amnon laughed. "You first have to have it, then you can do without."

"I know. Only the best, and who needs it."

As if to prove it, he put on jeans and tennis shoes, and so did I. We took the metro, ate in a cheap bistro, walked under bridges, got soaked in the rain and walked into Cartier's. He bought me their famous triple-ring and slipped it on my wet finger.

"It looks like a wedding ring," I said.

"A triple one, enjoy it."

On the way back, in the taxi, I was crying. Pretending these were raindrops I was wiping my face.

"Moment of truth?" he asked. "I thought you were having fun."

For the first time I wanted it all to last, his wife to disappear, his past and mine to be erased and for us to last. I was crying now and he was helpless and kind. On the way we stopped for the newspapers.

The headlines in big print said, "Emergency Declared, General Mobilization. Egyptian Army Moving Toward The Frontier." Amnon diverted the taxi to the El Al office; he walked in to the manager to get us on the first flight home. I went on to the hotel to pack.

The phone was ringing in the room and Amnon was on the line.

"Pack and pay and check out. There is some money in the camera case. Grab a taxi and go to Orly, I'll wait there at the El Al stand."

"Is it that bad?"

"Better to find out in Lydda than be stuck here." As an afterthought he added, "As pleasant as it is here."

I threw everything into the two suitcases, figuring we could sort it out later. I forgot the bathrobes hanging behind the bathroom door, and called for a bellboy. Paid, grabbed for a taxi, bid our love nest farewell, promising myself to return, and got to Orly. Amnon was waiting on the pavement boarding cards in hand. We had time to check in and walk to the gate soberly.

"I didn't have time to ask you," he started, "but if you'd rather stay a few days you are welcome to be my guest. I may be exaggerating, but if my men are called I'd better be there."

"You must be crazy to think I would want to stay."

"It was a good party."

"The best."

On the flight home we didn't talk much. As if not to impose words on something beautiful we both treasured.

Below, while the sun set and we seemed static, Europe was flying, gently unfolding greens of forests and whites of snow peaks, untroubled blues of lakes and seas.

It was getting dark, dinner was served and left untouched.

"It isn't Lassere," he laughed.

"Where did you learn all these things?"

"The Fancy College. It's nonsense. A matter of selection until you reach the top and dismiss the others. Tips, guidebooks, fancy friends, experience. You grow tired of the finesse after a while, and settle for the knowledge without the need to use it."

"It's also costly."

"Who's counting? It's nice to own good things if you manage not to worry about them, as long as you know you can do without."

I kept turning the triple-ring on my finger. He was already with "his men, his tanks."

"Another war? Do you think?"

"It seems inevitable, but we'll soon find out. We are in good shape now, ready to go."

"You sound as if you want a war."

"Don't be righteous about it. All that stuff about young kids getting killed and war widows and orphans. When fighting is the answer for something, we want to fight. A good victory prevents bloodshed, even if people are killed. I've settled for the fact that we'll always have wars, every few years, and this will go on for a long time.

"It sounds horrible."

"Yes. A no-choice life."

We flew over Cyprus and soon after the captain announced the Israeli coastline. The lights of Tel-Aviv were spread out on both sides of the aircraft. Someone started singing and clapping and others joined. I had unwanted tears in my eyes, pride and fear of home-coming mixed with the thought of separation from Amnon. He was giving me instructions now.

"I'll put you in a cab. You take both suitcases and sort them out at home. I'll send for mine tomorrow. I'll go home to get my uniform and join my unit. Will try to call you as soon as I can."

"I am a reservist, too, you know. I'll report tomorrow to my unit."

"Don't play hero. I want you safe and well when this is over."

"The same to you."

We were taxiing along the runway and stopped in front of the building. The door swung open and a whiff of orange blossom hit the inside of the plane. I took a deep breath.

"The best perfume in the world," he smiled.

"I thought Guerlain's Chamade was."

"Forget it."

The scent filled me with unexpected joy. It was spring and there were wild flowers everywhere. I thought of the storks and seagulls flying back to Europe, and the lemon tree in blossom in the garden of my house. We didn't kiss. He held my hand for a moment. I whispered, "Take care," and he walked away.

I waited long for the suitcases and it was long after midnight when I arrived at my apartment. I folded his things neatly in his case and closed it.

CHAPTER 7

The country woke up on October 24, 1973, a Wednesday, as if it were a wedding day. Cease-fire was expected at any moment, and the words, "The war is over," though not yet uttered by anybody, were ringing in every heart. The radio announced that cease-fire would be effective at 0700 hours. Our forces in the city of Suez's outskirts isolated the 3rd Army and cut off all communicating roads between Cairo and Suez. The U.N. was preparing to establish observation posts along the cease-fire lines.

It was a question of hours. The battle around the city of Suez was still on but the rest of the front was quiet. Occasional nervous shots only confirmed that for all practical and emotional purposes the war was over.

On the last day of war I functioned mechanically. My head felt empty of analysis or assessment, and I couldn't touch any food. Tears held back for long weeks flowed easily now, and from time to time I carelessly wiped my wet face. My mother must have taken the children out, for they were not there when I woke up.

I had had plans for this day. I thought of the cake

I had planned to bake, the bottle of champagne we would open. I was going to stay home and awake with the children and celebrate. Now it was emptiness and solitude with two vague thoughts settling in. No. 7 was still there, his identity bound to be discovered as he is about to die. The other thought was of Avi. I had grown newly fond of him. We had a language together, and had formed an attachment. I felt a slight pain thinking of his departure.

I drove to the hospital as if nothing had changed and only a few days later it occurred to me that on this long last day the memory or absence of Daniel, my husband, hadn't crossed my mind.

There was no champagne, not much joy either. Relief, some tears, a lot of words, arguments, disbelief at moments and mostly fatigue.

The Professor seemed exhausted for once. So did Leib, who sat with Julie in the hall. The public phone didn't stop ringing, but people were less eager to receive calls. It seemed as if the glue had started melting. The big family around the radios and TV sets, with the staff and the relatives, the volunteers, the U.J.A. ladies' missions, the social workers and the entertainers, this big family didn't really exist. Suddenly there were just individuals. Patients rather than heroes, worried about their itching and bandages and uncertain futures. The tension and the public drama were to disappear soon, they sensed it already. They would remain invalids. Struggling, malfunctioning, unhappy reminders of a terrible war.

"Did your husband call?" Shula asked me.

"Who?"

"Daniel. Your husband. He is across the canal, isn't he?"

"Yes. No, he didn't call. Anything new in room 7?" I went to see him. No change, only that whatever life there was in him seemed to be floating away. The room was as close to an empty room as a place with someone in it can be. Hope gone, too, there was only the smell.

Avi, too, asked me whether Daniel called. I felt awkward. As if I had joined the club too late. I now belonged to the directly involved, only the involvement didn't mean danger anymore. I entered the theater when the play was over; I arrived in time for the curtain calls.

Having been asked, I wondered why Daniel hadn't called, but there were too many acceptable explanations so I let it go.

Avi told me about Nadav. His family came to visit during the day. So did his girlfriend. Nadav tried to explain to her that he was deformed under the silver sulfadiazine and bandage. She wouldn't take him seriously, tried to joke and pretend that she couldn't care less. He asked her not to come again and when she wouldn't listen, he shouted and ordered her out. He then undid the dressing, as painful as it was (and utterly forbidden), grinding his teeth.

His mother almost fainted. The sight was both terrifying and nauseating. He asked his father to get him a mirror and the old man obeyed him. Avi rang for the nurse. Nadav was in ghastly pain. He glanced at the mirror and threw it on the floor when the nurse entered in panic. Another nurse took the parents out and the Professor explained to them the plastic surgery technique while Nadav was re-dressed and sedated. Later a psychologist came, thinking she had to calm Avi, too. Breakdowns are infectious, you know. She was young and pretty, the psychologist, and Avi embarrassed her by looking at her breasts and playing dumb. Tomorrow they'll parade in nose and ear cases from the Six Day War, a living proof to the miraculous advance of plastic surgery.

The Professor asked the staff into his room. He mumbled a few words about "the day we have all been waiting for," and then explained clearly that for us, in white, the war wasn't over yet. The cease-fire would cause depression in the patients, they might feel left out once the attention dwindles, and it was our duty, the staff and the volunteers who could continue for a while, not to let them fall into self-pity and despair. "Normal life will resume," he said. "For them the fight is still a long one, and they need our help and care and love more than before. Now they are heroes, next week they will be handicapped bums, rejected lovers, fighting shame and loneliness."

End of speech, nods of agreement, slight embarrassment at potential accusations.

Later he addressed me separately. Night duty wouldn't be necessary anymore as we don't expect emergencies. If I could come during the day for a few hours he'd appreciate it. Also, would I remind the major in charge of absentees and the unidentified of No. 7 in our ward?

The sudden exhaustion that engulfed the ward affected me, too.

Avi's bell was buzzing. Nadav was still asleep and

Avi woke up. Water was the excuse, but he didn't seem sleepy.

"Well, Sister," he said as if addressing a meeting. "It is good-bye for us?"

"Don't be silly. Go to sleep. I won't leave this ward before you do."

"Only when we do, one of us has something to go back to."

"The other still has a choice. Isn't that what you always wanted, the freedom to choose?"

"Is it? Did I really choose to return here, or did I simply have to? Not that fighting wars is more meaningful than the research I'm supposed to do next."

"Meaningful is for the boy scouts. Here it's a life, some kind of life. Mostly hysterical and loaded with self-importance. You still have a choice. You also have parents, a wife, a child."

"They'll all go back. Julie will tell her Springfield psychiatrist all about it. Did you see how Leib blushes when he sees her?"

"Maybe she like him. They seem to have something in common."

"Please believe me, I don't care. This hospital bed makes one, made me, very self-centered. I've been spending whole days thinking of my body, my wounds, my recovery, my scars and now—my future."

"You can get out of bed in a wheelchair now, pretty soon on your feet. You have enough time to figure out what next."

He changed the subject. "Your husband will return soon. What will your life be like?"

"Daniel didn't go south for the war. He thought

they could use him when the fighting was over." I tiptoed toward the door.

"Please don't leave me."

"I'm tired, we'll talk later."

"I mean don't leave tomorrow or the day after."

"Good-night."

I told Shula I could be found on the bench in the garden. I needed air. I sat there shivering in spite of the wind jacket, trying to convince myself that the war that was over had lasted only a few weeks. It wasn't a lifetime, it wasn't one cycle over and a new one about to begin, but just an interval after which everything resumes.

An interval which caused all sophistication to disappear. The small things seemed meaningless—a headache, a bad meal, an unpleasant remark by someone, being cold, or hot, or uncomfortable, being tired or bored, it was all trivial. Everything that constitutes the normal flow of everyday sensations, not activities, was pushed away. The big things weren't there either. The big words and the profound thoughts, philosophic attitudes and deep convictions, these, too, were put aside. There was just existence; life itself acquired an importance, no matter which rules or standards or codes you lived by. The only morality was to be, and the rest belonged to memories or hopes which could not be placed in terms of definite time. As if war were an independent life cycle, from birth to death, with new boundaries encircling thoughts, feelings and actions, provisory but unbreakable.

On Yom Kippur, when the war started, all my thoughts were turned to Amnon. As if all the evils of all wars and battles could be summed up in his death.

And he was killed in another war that was supposed to be the last war.

Only it was summer then. And I was with a unit in the Sinai with not much to do except move onward with my commander, take messages, write notes, work on his diary and jump from the half-track to a ditch whenever everybody else did. We weren't that much younger, only that fast victory is a youthful experience. We were joking and laughing and the songs on the radio were pompous and happy. On the fourth day of the war we were deep into the Sinai, our forces were approaching the canal, and in spite of the casualties, there was an exhilarating sensation of superman ability. On that night Amnon died. His tank was hit, and what he said could never happen to him, just did. At dawn, when we met with the division he belonged to, I heard of his death.

I was sitting on my kit-bag eating apricots which had been flown down to us with other fresh supplies. Next to me two generals conferred with my commander; I wasn't listening until I heard Amnon's surname mentioned. It was followed by the briefest moment of silence, the respectful silence you give to the brave dead even in the midst of a battle talk.

When they left, I asked my commander. He confirmed what I had heard.

"Did you know him? They say he was quite a guy. Didn't have to pop his head out under fire though."

What could I tell him? That Amnon didn't believe it could happen to him, that we were lovers, that we had just returned from Paris together, that our love story had to end anyway and that's one way stories end?

So I cried. It was hot and dry and the tears mixed with the dust that covered my face to from a muddy mask. I cried, and carried on with whatever I was supposed to do, and wiped my nose and tears and we drove on and I thought there will be no end to my crying unless something will help me stop it.

The something was someone. Daniel, then a stranger, came to report to the commander and stopped near me with concern. Which made me cry louder. I don't know what helped him guess, unless it is obvious that girls don't cry in war because they have lost a pair of earrings or a job.

"Someone you love was killed?" It was a statement. I stopped crying. I nodded and took the box of Kleenex and the cigarette he offered me.

My feet were numb and the bench was wet. I returned to the ward. Everyone, really everyone, was fast asleep. Out of habit, the radio was still switched on, broadcasting light music.

I drove into town in the morning. A brisk wind slapped the pavements and tossed the leaves in aimless circles. Very few people were around, and none too joyful. Along the beach some seagulls searched for prey and the sound of the towering waves somehow calmed me.

A policewoman approached my parked car. I must have looked terrible for she asked me if I were in trouble.

"No. The war is really over," I said. "Just relaxing."

"It's going to rain," she offered.

I drove on, not really wanting to go home, missing Daniel as part of the sudden normalcy imposed on us.

"So," my mother welcomed me when I opened the door. "That's it." Her short statements always offended me somehow. She continued, "Now you can tend to your children, put some weight on. Daniel will be home soon, back to the routine."

"It's not over in the hospital."

"It is in the library. I have to be back to work, normal hours."

"Who would want to read books now?"

"Whoever did before. Don't be dramatic. It isn't the first nor the last war and—other than the dead and their families—people will emerge unmarked."

Perhaps she was right. The papers wrote of trauma and an earthquake. Accusations flew in all directions. But perhaps my square mother was right; in her organized brain cells lay truth, sharp and simple.

"Someone named Julie telephoned. A major from Absentees left a number. Shula called to say the Professor's son-in-law was killed just before the cease-fire. What are your plans now?"

I wasn't listening. I could see the Professor's tired face twist in pain, a pain that remains on faces of the bereaved for the rest of their lives.

"Are you going back there tonight?" she repeated.

"Just to visit. I'll be working in the mornings now. I'll send the children to school, and when they are away I'll be in the ward, that's all. I need some sleep now." From my bedroom I called the major. He was friendly and anxious to talk.

"We may have found a clue to the guy in your
ward you seemed to care about."

"No. 7?"

"Is that what you call him? A landlady in Beer-
Sheba called this morning. Wondering about someone
who rented a room in her house. He sent himself
letters for a while, then stopped. He had no relatives,
an odd fellow."

"What makes you think that may be him?"

"Just a hunch. Maybe simply because I can't accept
the fact that nobody had identified him for so long.
She is sending the letters and some of his stuff with
one of my men. I can bring it to the ward tonight."

"Thanks for calling me."

"Don't mention it. I've noticed your concern. It must
have bothered you. And the Professor, too."

"He lost his son-in-law yesterday."

"I'm sorry."

Then the silence following the news. How often
did we sense its heaviness these weeks, and found
no way to break it. A silence at the end of chatter,
where words had no meaning, between the verbal
message and the pain.

I called Julie in her hotel. She was waiting for the
call, wanted to know if she could bring her daughter,
Karen, over in the afternoon.

"She should meet some children, she's lonely for
company." Later, she said, I could drive them both
to the hospital. She might stay the night helping Leib
sort out his papers, and the child would return with
her grandparents.

I said all right, mechanically, to everything. I
wanted to sleep and I wasn't really listening.

When I woke up the house looked like a birthday party. My own boys played with Avi's child, the neighbor's children baked cookies with my mother and Julie, and toys, drawings, records and picture books were all over the place.

I smiled. It felt good. The austere mood of the past weeks must have affected the children. In the best of times my mother couldn't tolerate disorder, but in honor of our guests she let it go. The house felt warm and the cookies in the oven had a wonderful smell. The boys were loud and laughing and their kisses tasted like the raspberry juice they had just drunk. For a brief second I pretended this was my life, a kettle on the stove, something in the oven, two lovely children, a loving husband who would soon be back, green plants in pots, helpful mother, friendly neighbor, a secure if unexciting nest. I pretended the rest was fringes. The living memory of Amnon, myself the way I used to be, my hidden fancies and the hospital.

My brother Boaz called. He will not be coming home soon. He was on the Golan Heights. Now that the war is over, he likes it there. He had things to do, and in particular didn't want to face the hysterical civilian routine.

My brother was a proof of the invalidity of genetics. He was unlike anybody in the family. He was as opposed to my mother's orderly being as anyone could be, and had none of the sensitivity and warmth of my father. He never communicated with me either. His world was woven of dreams and wild fancies; the unexpected constituted his routine. He never held a job, or a friend, never accomplished anything more

than merely existing. The term "family" seemed to
have had no meaning for him. He was a nomad without being nervous, placid yet interested in extremes,
helpful and generous without caring or loving.

Julie wanted to talk and we took the teacup to
my bedroom.

"I'm leaving in a couple of days."

I looked at her. The face was lively without being
intelligent, the eyes soft but not kind. She was a
foreigner.

"I thought you wanted to stay, to find things to do."

"It's not my scene. With Avi it will never work,
and the rest of you I can admire but not understand."

"You get along well with Leib, there will be other
friends."

"What for?"

I shrugged. She was right. It wasn't her scene.

"You are all too involved with something that means
little to me. A destiny. It's like masturbation. You
analyze yourselves, you relive your history, you talk
in big words of fate and identity and you dig into
your collective souls every moment of the day. It
may be heroic and commendable and noble. To me
it's just frightening, inhuman."

"If I remember right, that's one of the reasons Avi
left."

"It's in him, too. He doesn't talk much of heritage
and sources, and he is less pompous about being
chosen people. So he takes a Valium a day and acts
like a regular boy, but his bearded ancestors with
their sense of mission are trailing him hopelessly."

"And here, do you feel it here, in a home? Don't
you see we live a life, like anywhere else?"

"Not really. The war is over so you celebrate, and it feels phony to me. You playact the happy family. Your mother wears a smile, your husband is away, and you can't wait to go back to the hospital."

Maybe she was perceptive, maybe she was wrong. I wasn't in the mood to argue a hopeless point.

We drove to the ward. She was leaving in a couple of days, taking Karen with her. Avi's parents would follow in a week, and Avi would make up his mind when he was ready.

The major from Absentees was there waiting, a short jovial fellow, trying with harmless humor to balance the tragic job he had to cope with. He was holding a leather case that looked like a worn schoolbag, and I wondered how many shattered hopes were packed into it.

His handshake was firm and warm. I thought of Julie's description of our inhuman self-infatuation.

The Professor was locked in his room. He didn't want to go home, or see anybody, and we let him be.

We walked to room 7, the quietest corner in the ward, and shut the door.

He fumbled with the lock of his case and pulled out an envelope. We both glanced at the dying man as if we were going to deliver the news to him.

"Not too much, but something. The landlady from Beer-Sheba delivered this. She looked at our photographs and said the build and size matched. Not much to go by. The man she claimed missing had been a tenant of hers for less than a year. She wasn't sure about his job. He said his name was Arik Berkov. Paid rent promptly and was absent often. Until the war he never received mail, but on Yom Kippur he left in

uniform and every few days a letter arrived for him.
She knew his handwriting and figured he was writing
to himself from somewhere. Then it stopped, and a
few days ago she entered the room. She found this
diary on the desk"—he pointed to a brown notebook—
"and an envelope for her with a month's rent. She
wasn't sure whether to report anything, for if he had
no family, it would be only natural that he should
stay wherever he was and not rush to her to report.
She had a hunch, though, felt it was her duty, as she
put it, and brought the papers to our southern office."

"Did you read it all?"

"Yes. You will, too. We have no right, you know.
He may show up tomorrow and claim we invaded his
privacy. I have to go. We'll talk after you've read it
all. The real riddle is something else. I checked with
the central computer of the army, then with ministry
of interior. There isn't an Arik Berkov registered anywhere. There isn't a soldier by that name, nor a citizen.
No identity papers were ever issued bearing this
name."

He looked puzzled, like a schoolboy facing an
impossible equation.

"I'm not a detective," I said. "I am bothered, curious,
disturbed, but I don't see how I can help. For all we
know there is someone around who adopted a name
for some convenience, and there is No. 7 here who may
have nothing to do with Arik Berkov."

"There is something else. I asked the landlady some
questions. She clearly remembers the Paul Valéry
book. Once when she was tidying the room, he asked
her about *Monsieur Teste*. He was very anxious not to
lose it."

"Why would he go under a false name?"

"It's in the diary. Not the name he chose, but the motivation."

"Do you have other cases of unidentified persons?"

"Not alive. One died in Hadassah Hospital in Jerusalem. There are many missing in battle. There are no lists of prisoners yet from Syria or Egypt. There are unidentified corpses temporarily buried, of which we have photographs and fingerprints."

"What difference does it make?" I asked him, bitterly.

"Whether we know who this fellow is, or let him die nameless?"

"He is as good as dead. If by a miracle he lives, there is no enigma. If he dies, and it doesn't affect any living person, why bother?"

"Principle, I suppose. We can only think and act according to our own set of references. We value human life and the personality behind the name. A question of our own dignity, I suppose."

I thought of Julie's verdict.

"There is a girl here. An American. She says she can't stand our preoccupation with ourselves. We give life an outsize dimension."

"The American army would have acted the same way. It's also true that we don't have an 'Unknown Soldier' monument."

"Don't give me the 'We are, after all, one small family' bit."

"No. Perhaps she is right, but then, that's the way it is. We are aggressive and dramatic about ourselves, and I don't mind."

I thought of him going home in the evening. Wearing slippers and civilian clothes. I was sure he washed dishes wearing an apron and watered the flowers in the little garden.

"Do you have children?"

"Daughters. Three girls. One is in the army, North Headquarters. Considering my job, I secretly wonder whether I shouldn't be grateful for having no sons in the army."

He smiled awkwardly, apologetic for what he just said. He knew I had two sons.

"How is the husband?"

"Down in Sinai. Helping gather the pieces, logistics of Beni's division or something."

"We should get together one evening, when he is back. My wife bakes a good apple strudel."

We agreed to be in touch after I had read the diary and letters, and I saw him to his car. The Professor's door was open now, but the room was empty.

I managed to get the southern command operator through the hospital exchange. She connected me to Beni's Headquarters. "It's an overseas call," she joked. "They are in Africa." Two more operators and I had Beni on the line. He had the hoarse deep voice of a man who hasn't slept for weeks. He also spoke very slowly, pronouncing each of the three syllables of my name separately and with a touch of surprise.

"Thanks for letting Daniel join us. He is priceless."

"He didn't exactly ask permission. How is he? How are you?"

"Victorious. It's also beautiful here, like a tropical resort. You should come and visit. Fresh dates are in season." He talked as if he were on vacation on some exotic island.

"Is Daniel around?"

"Not this moment. I'll have him call back, are you at home?"

"No, in the hospital. He knows the number. Is he well?"

"Putting on weight. Are you still beautiful and silent?"

"Beautiful I never was. Silent? No more. Give my love." We hadn't seen each other much. He visited when Ofer was born, and called once in a while afterward.

In the war in which Amnon was killed, Beni was commanding a brigade and Daniel was with him. I wondered whether this was his last war, and could almost see him under a palm tree in Africa, talking slowly and puffing on his pipe.

For the next two hours I wasn't able to get as much as a glance at the precious envelope the major left with me. The phone was ringing incessantly, a stream of visitors arrived, each staying a little while longer to discuss the cease-fire. An impatient mood prevailed in the ward, as if they were all going home the following day.

I tried to avoid Avi. He was in the midst of a serious conflict, having to make a major decision. My presence encouraged his cynicism, and what he had to figure out had to be done with honesty.

Nadav had a visitor from O.R.T. He was offered a training course as an instructor in the technical school from which he had graduated. He wanted to share his pride. Sharing one emotion or another seemed to be my lot that night. As if they all sought the attention which was bound to dwindle in the next few days.

After midnight the pace slowed. The patients were asleep and the visitors gone. I wanted to read the diary but the bell rang from one of the rooms. It was the "Arab Room." I seldom went inside. Shula was asleep now and I decided to see if I could help.

The military policeman at the door greeted me.

"The colonel is in terrible pain. Perhaps you should call the doctor."

I went in. The night lamp threw dim light on the beds. The sergeant was asleep next to the window and the colonel's face was twisted. He was suffering. He spoke a few words of English and tried to smile when he saw me. I said I'd call the doctor and he thanked me in Arabic.

Most of the wounded prisoners were in a hospital apart, attached to ours but a few minutes away in a camp converted for the purpose. The severe cases which needed special treatments were in the regular wards, guarded and isolated.

When they first arrived there was curiosity and animosity. When the war took a bad turn a few angry fists were pointed in the direction of the "Arab Room," but there was no communication. The doctors did their job, devoted to human life regardless of origin, and the other patients were too involved with their own suffering. Occasionally a curious visitor wanted to enter, to see what the enemy was like, but they had to admit that these two patients were no different. Their condition was grave, and pity rather than compassion motivated the nurses who treated them.

This room was merely another reminder of the futility of the fight. There they lay, one dying, next to their victims, all at the mercy of medical ingenuity and hoping to emerge alive and resume a life. They felt safe here. One day they would return home in exchange for our own prisoners. This little room was their world. They talked, listened to the radio, ate the food they were not used to, watched TV and wrote home. On my part there was no curiosity, no hatred, and no sympathy. I went to look for Leib, who hurried with a syringe.

"I doubt whether he'll live," he said, "his kidneys are in bad shape. I may call Rothman later."

I wasn't listening. It was too late to call Daniel, I thought, and wasn't sure whether I really wanted to. He knew where to reach me if he cared to.

I put the diary away to read later, and opened the letters. A person writing to himself. I couldn't avoid thinking of him as unbalanced, perhaps mad. Maybe the whole thing had to do with a lunatic. Not too dumb, considering the Paul Valéry book, but truly disturbed.

There were two letters. Dated the first two days of the war. The handwriting was ordinary, regular, easy to read. The lined paper was torn from a copybook. There was no opening or signature, just a brief acknowledgment of existence, like clues in mud at the end of a road.

"Joined a new unit, most of the men are reservists. I don't know anybody, and am unknown to them. We are being driven west, straight to the front line so the paperwork will be done later. Too bad winter started early this year, but we were issued warm socks and underwear. As usual, my fear of killing is stronger than that of being killed. The men are very noisy and nervous. It feels strange to operate in company rather than alone."

The second note was similar. The writing less orderly, as if written in haste and discomfort.

"During the night we were shelled. We dug in and waited, advanced, shot some in the dark and found cover by daylight. We've seen armor divisions advancing and spreading but there seems to be little logic to the whole thing. I don't know whether we are defending or attacking. The commander is awaiting orders and seems confused. I feel out of place but this may change with daylight when we know the score."

I felt desperately disappointed. If the diary was more of the same, there was very little to find out.

Julie was curled in the armchair in the waiting room. Asleep. I covered her with a thin blanket and she awoke startled.

"Oh, it's you. Thanks."

"Sorry. I didn't mean to wake you."

"All the better. You saved me from the end of a terrible dream."

Reluctantly, I offered her coffee. I didn't seek company and Julie's young freshness enervated me—a touch of jealousy mixed with the memory of what I had been like with Amnon. Pretty and smart and competent, she found our pains and wounds "admirable" and our bravery "fascinating" and I felt clumsy and aged. I felt she was sensitive to my thoughts.

"I have no business watching you all. That's why

I'm going tomorrow. Avi doesn't need me and this place, at this time, is only for the contributors."

"You may come back, when things are different."

"Will they ever be?"

"Sure. Two years after a war, a couple of years before a war, we are quite normal."

She was tense, perhaps merely tired.

"It's the 'waiting' mentality. You, Shula, your mother, all the women I met. You don't live a life, you are waiting, vigilant, lingering."

"Are we? Waiting for what?"

"Waiting for your men to go and waiting for them to return. First you waited for the fathers, hoping to reach adulthood with both parents alive, then you got married and waited for the husbands to do their turn and come back safely alive, or in one piece. Then the sons, watching them grow up, counting the years till they are eighteen and it's their time to go and return, and by then other young women are also waiting for them and preparing to bear their children and wait for them. It's like an emergency hospital where you all wait for the next red lamp above the door to the operation room and watch to see who is wheeled out alive and who is sacrificed in the process."

"And the in-betweens?"

"In between there are reservists coming and going, accidents on maneuvers, graves to visit and widows and orphans to tend to. In between you knit warm socks for the next war and air the shelters, and listen to the news like maniacs. Those who dare leave the waiting room are ostracized. But you stick together best when danger is imminent and wonder who will be next on the casualty list. As if every woman is a potential widow and every child a potential orphan."

"You are leaving tomorrow," I muttered. "I can't even prove you wrong. Why should I bother? Invite you to take trips with us, see what joy we have in life, show you what was built and achieved and created, invite you to partake in our ordinary happiness and banal quarrels, prove our sanity? You are miles off target, and it's not the time and place to tell you where to aim."

Leib was asleep on the bed next to the wall, or so I thought. He must have half-listened for he removed the blanket from his face and spoke to me.

"Do you love your boys?"

"What a question! More than anything in the world."

"And when you see other mothers' boys burnt and maimed in this ward, doesn't it bother you? Don't you just want to take yours away from here, and escape somewhere where they'll be safe?"

"You must be joking. Escape where? To the Fiji Islands to play with glass beads and eat bananas? To Manhattan to worry about them whenever they take the subway? To Europe where between the art treasures and the culture and the dreadful climate they'll be reminded of their being Jewish occasionally, as if it were leprosy, mostly cured, but still present in blood tests? I love my boys, and I love Daniel, and because of my love I am here. And because of our love we have to fight occasionally, and this too will have an end."

This abstract conversation was leading nowhere. We were all exaggerating, trying to be articulate. I

claimed I had some work to do, and Julie and Leib
continued to talk as I left the room.

I walked among the beds to the pale light from outside. Another dawn. My last one in the ward. If there
was another war, I was going to stay home. I needed
the children, even if they managed well without me.
There will always be enough volunteers making beds
and holding hands. So for me it was the last war. I
smiled to myself, remembering Daniel's saying, "Maturity is to know when you are superfluous!" He said
it referring to himself, and yet he was with Beni,
across the Suez Canal, and I was in Ward L, and at
times like this we should have both been home clutching each other.

I said good-bye to Julie. She moved to kiss me but I
extended my hand and we left it at that. Leib was
staying. "No, not forever," he said. Just until he felt
his services were no longer required. When the medical staff in the field returned to their regular posts,
he would resume his.

We both avoided saying, "Until the next time."

I told Avi and Nadav not to expect me that night,
doubting that anyone did, and took the brown envelope home with me.

The children were just ready to leave for school.
"Did I love them?" Leib had asked. Was he suggest-
ing I didn't? Did I do them wrong by taking hospital
duty? It wasn't really relevant. Here they were, both
my sons, a part of me, and we had a long way to
share. Whatever they missed now, I could make up
for later. They would grow to understand that love

isn't measured by the number of hours spent together. When Daniel is back, we should talk about a third child. He knew how much I wanted a daughter.

My mother was packing her things into a large canvas bag, folding each item carefully into plastic bags.

"Julie," she said. "Avi's wife."

"What about her?"

"Is she as clever as she is pretty?"

"I suppose so. Well trained in overanalyzing. Things she encounters should have meanings, and the meaning should mean something additional, and so forth. It can become exhausting."

"A result of leisure coupled with high education."

Mother left, saying something about hoping I'd manage on my own as her own duties had been neglected. I felt quite good being alone in my own home. She returned to her two-room apartment. She had no maid (Am I too old to wash eighty square meters of tiled floor?) and seldom went out in the evening (Nothing better than a good book). Was she, too, a waiting woman? Was it now the son-in-law she was waiting for—her own son back on the Golan Heights because he liked it better than her fastidious company—or was she already watching my sons grow, wondering when their turn would come? Julie's speech was a mind-twister. Somewhere between heart and guts I had to agree with her, but my answer came all from the head. Still, I didn't think of my sons as future soldiers or potential casualties.

When I loved Amnon I gave no thought to the possibility of his death in battle. Daniel I met in war, and together we dreamed of a red-roofed house and pots of jasmine on the windowsill. The boys were so small and young, I could easily afford thinking of peace in their lifetime, if I had to think of it at all.

With a cup of coffee and a sandwich, I settled on the sofa and opened the brown envelope. I didn't plan to read it now, just leaf through.

I was really looking for names, any name which would be real enough, with a face and a phone number to get me on a road which might lead somewhere. About halfway through the quick reading I stopped with a jolt. There was the name Daniel, just *Daniel*. I hurried down the page . . . then the initials D.D. He was referring to my husband!

From the little I had read it was obvious that our No. 7, if this were he, was someone with a borrowed identity, drafted for a job that had to be done and forgotten. There was something terrifying about the diary, the little I could understand of it. There was no warmth, no human contacts. A person working hard to sever attachments, to erase footmarks. A phantom, doing something, then evaporating and making sure no traces were left.

Daniel's name, if it were my Daniel, explained the fact that Arik Berkov was a name unlisted anywhere. Daniel had been what we termed jokingly, "a spy in Europe." He had worked with teams of operators. Though an unamusing coincidence, this could easily be one of them.

There were vague indications of relationships in Israel and in Europe, but they were mentioned only in order to be crossed off a list. The man, whoever he was, was working hard at being a loner, almost a nobody, yet there was no death wish, nor was he a failure.

There were no evaluations of people, no superlatives or even adjectives. A cold account of a life trying to diminish its significance to the minimum possible. He was completely unconcerned with his own predicament.

Then, strangely, the last few pages were different. The writer had discovered something new. Some of the apathy was gone. He was referring to a girl named O. He wrote about desert plants and even mentioned the beauty of sunsets. A few lines indicated the need to look for a job and there were apologetic words concerning a previous job, his mother, someone called G.

I knew I should give the diary to someone. I had no right to read it, and if I were right about his being an agent, it might even be classified. I decided to talk to Daniel and was sure he'd tell me what to do.

I put the diary aside, beginning to have qualms about my ability to comprehend. It was frightening and at the same time intriguing. Daniel, my husband, that was a different matter. I thought I knew him well, but I realized how little I knew about him.

CHAPTER 8

I wasn't at all tired. I planned not to go to work that evening. My mother had left the apartment impeccably clean, and lunch for the children was all prepared.

I sat and looked at the familiar living room. A low coffee table, four armchairs and a sofa, embroidered cushions and a whitewashed wall with two original paintings and a few lithographs. Yet, as my eyes examined the objects, I felt strangely out of place. As if the past few weeks had been spent in limbo, as if I were waking up from anesthesia, coming back to life from a shelter. I realized the paradox. I had escaped the war by plunging into the horrors of it. The burnt limbs and faces, the amputees, the invalids, the dead, they became abstract in the nightly duty, and the sound of guns and shells, the diving of aircraft and the roar of tanks advancing—this reality was so far away—sounds overcome and numbed by the silence of hospital corridors. I knew a terrible event had taken place, but I didn't feel it. People died, but I didn't know them. We claimed a victory, but I didn't rejoice in it, and when we were defeated at the beginning, I wasn't frightened. As if I weren't

really there. I wasn't even sure about the date or
the day of the week.

I picked up the newspaper. The Red Cross was
trying to obtain a list of prisoners of war. The Israeli
army sent medicines and plasma to the surrounded
Egyptian 3rd Division. Women volunteers were asked
to distribute mail. There were maps of the cease-fire
lines and I vaguely guessed where Beni's Headquarters was located.

I looked at the ads. A black Great Dane answering
to the name Tet was missing, a reward offered. A
white convertible Subaru stolen, another reward.
Three weddings and two Bar Mitzvahs postponed.
Announcements of nightclubs reopening. A fashion
show in the Sheraton Hotel, all profits to the Soldier's
Fund. Free entrance to soldiers at the Opera House
(*The Barber of Seville*). Cigarette manufacturers
apologizing for shortages caused by giving priority
to the front.

I changed to a flannel dressing gown and put the
uniform in the washing machine. I filled a bath and
washed my hair, and for the sense of luxury rubbed
some moisturizing cream on my face. From the mirror
an adult woman looked back at me. Not wrinkled
or marked by time, just mature, like at the end of
a chapter. Something was over and my face expressed
it. A resignation. Acceptance rather than aspiration.

As if the things never done, emotions never felt,
sensations never experienced were to remain in the
"never" category. It used to be a game I played with
myself. Listing all the "nevers." I have never had
champagne (Amnon thought it overrated). I have
never taken a cruise or been on an island. I have

never screamed in horror, never made love to a
stranger. It was a long and mostly frivolous list, and
nothing on it could be classed as a serious deprivation.
I also didn't have a secret. Something hilariously good
or frightfully bad that was hidden deep in me that
I wished no one to know about. No heroism either.
Every man I knew could tell battle stories and they
all had heroic moments. They had been shot at and
advanced under fire, they had saved a friend from
death, they had rescued a wounded commander or
taken a hill single-handed. Not that they boasted,
but they had a moment of heroism to recall, to justify
lesser moments, to casually tell their sons about. When
I took hospital duty, I half-entertained the thought of
such heroic moments involving myself. To be the only
one around to notice a failing heartbeat, or a block
in an important lifesaving infusion. To help someone
will himself to a full recovery in spite of expectations.
This never happened. The trained nurses were there,
watchful and alert. Leib was always there, and all
the instruments and machinery worked without fail.
Our only failure was No. 7, and though I concentrated
my ambition and intelligence and heart on him, all
I could manage was to gather a few pieces of information which, even when deciphered, couldn't help
him regain consciousness.

The phone rang for a while before I picked it up.
It was Julie, calling from the airport.

"Another good-bye," she said. "There is a delay in
the flight. Did I wake you?"

"No. Just thinking about all the things I've never
done."

"Try the opposite. I'm sure it makes an impressive list."

"Sure. Have a good trip home."

"I'm calling to say I'll be back. I know, because I find it very difficult to leave."

"But you are leaving."

"I'm trying to be honest. None of you said, 'Please stay.'"

"And if we did?"

"I would have stayed."

"You would still regard it as an adventure."

"Yes, but without guilt. Home is no paradise either."

"You can do something about your life."

"We fall into a routine. Child, house-care, tennis, friends, make-believe activities. We count time to the moment when it will be true to say, 'It's too late to start now.'"

"You are young, and pretty, and intelligent."

"You sound like my mother-in-law. I am also selfish and lazy and—gosh. They are calling my flight! I'll come back soon."

"Please do. Shalom."

I could see her rushing to the departure gate, in blue denims and a large Vuitton carryall bag. Something between a Peeping Tom and an analyst. I wondered what made her and Avi split.

And what made Daniel and me stay together? What made us get married in the first place, share a life, be parents to two children?

It was need and affection on first sight, rather than love. Amnon was dead and I was crying over my loss when Daniel appeared. Not for fear of solitude, not because of a shattered future we could have had together, but rather pain felt at a physical disappearance. A body, a voice, laughter in the eyes, gestures of hands never to be seen or heard or felt again. We weren't one entity, and I wasn't halved by his death. I remained fully there, changed perhaps, but functioning, and Daniel understood it.

He wasn't overly gentle about it. He didn't join me for condolence. He respected my grief, but offered me a beginning of something new.

It was the end of the Six Day War. Romance was neither possible nor wanted. Courting meant a bar of chocolate, a fresh evening paper and two new pairs of khaki socks. On the third day after the war he brought his sleeping bag and smoothed the sand under mine. Our first double bed under starry Sinai sky, without touching. We smiled together rather than laughed, and we talked little about past or future. The war was over and reservists were returning home or going on leave. We stayed. It was safe and isolated, and the small world of brigade Headquarters offered comfort and protection.

Trucks arrived with fresh supplies, a helicopter brought mail and papers, tents were erected and we had facilities for washing and laundering. I had no desire to go anywhere. I did some paperwork, and Daniel was busy with postwar planning and logistics. We started peeling layers from each other when we were alone. We never mentioned Amnon or Daniel's girlfriend (Beni mentioned her casually one day and got a silencing look from Daniel), but we talked about our childhood and families.

It was like feeding a computer with data. To be

stored, classified and analyzed without sentiments or
unnecessary detail. Just information.

An army camp in the desert creates its own life
rhythm. Everybody and everything is silhouetted
clearly as if on an immense stage made of yellow
dunes, shifting slightly but lacking variety. No corners,
no doors to hide behind, no trees or bushes to escape
to, and every footstep, though soundless, leaves a
trace deeper than real size. When we wanted to be
alone, we climbed an empty damaged half-track. It
was a real treat to drive the jeep ten miles to where
the flat plateau ended and folded gently down to a
sunbaked plain.

Beni found out for me the date of Amnon's
funeral—or rather the transfer from a provisory
cemetery to one near his home. Daniel didn't say
anything when I mentioned I'd like to go north on
that day, merely offered to drive me there. "If we
have the time," he added, "we may go to Jerusalem
and see the Wall."

Amnon was to be buried in the fertile red soil
among orange orchards; his death gave us new
territories, a new united Jerusalem and an access to
the longed-for Wailing Wall. Or so they said, meaning, "It's worth it." The sacrifice was accepted and
rewarded, and I wondered then whether mothers and
wives and sons of the dead thought it was worth it.
Was it really easier to accept the absence of a dear
one, if one had the ancient stones of the Wall instead,
and the Golan Heights and this majestic desert we
camped in? These thoughts were irrelevant. It wasn't
a bargain one settled for beforehand. It was the way
things happened in war, uncalculated, inexplicable,

the total gain never to be measured against the loss of one life.

We took Beni's jeep to drive north. We crossed the old frontier, unmarked now, and breathed in the healthy smells of cow manure, fresh cornfields and barley stems after the harvest. With sunset we arrived in Tel-Aviv. The streets were crowded, traffic heavy as usual, and though many men were in uniform, the city felt as civilian as ever. There was so much to say and we talked so little. Daniel was to pick me up the next day at noon, drive to Jerusalem and try to make it back to Headquarters by night. He gave me his address and phone number, in case I changed my mind, and left me in front of my mother's house.

I didn't want to go back to my apartment. I was afraid of Amnon's presence there and perhaps a sense of guilt crept in, too. Homecoming was pleasant. My little brother, a young teen-ager then, wanted war stories, and my mother was all affection, cheesecake, chicken soup and herb shampoo thrown in.

I ate, bathed, chatted, but felt fidgety and restless. I sensed my mother's love and care, but she wasn't really the person I longed to be with. So I tried to be gentle about it. "I have to see whether my apartment is still there. I'll come tomorrow, we'll talk some more."

"But we have hardly seen you. There is so much to tell," she sighed.

She didn't nag or press, and I walked out of there leaving laundry behind and feeling rotten.

It was a short bus ride to Daniel's place. There was light in his window, and the dusty jeep was parked in front. Just before knocking on the door it occurred to me he might not be alone. If he had company—there was no sound—he didn't have to open. I tapped gently.

Daniel out of uniform looked older, more ordinary and very friendly. I started to apologize, but he gently put his hand to my mouth and then replaced it with his lips. I wasn't even annoyed by the fact that he expected me, and we walked to the bedroom as if we'd done it many times before.

I watched Amnon's burial from a distance, wearing a fresh uniform. There were many funerals in the military cemetery. The small group around the open grave were just faces to me. Rina dressed in a black skirt and blouse, two children, an array of uncles and aunts wiping tears and noses, and a guard of honor saluting the lowered corpse. The sound of soft earth being piled on and the colors of the wreaths from the unit and the chocolate factory made me feel slightly faint. I wanted to cry and couldn't, wanted to approach them and didn't. They were burying a part of themselves. I was an onlooker, burying a part of my past to be replaced by something else. For them he was irreplaceable.

Daniel met me at the cemetery gate. I was still holding the flowers I had bought when entering.

"You forgot the flowers," he said.

"I'll go alone some other time."

In all the years since we have never mentioned Amnon's name, and though his memory rested with me, vivid and painful at times, it never hovered between us.

On the way to Jerusalem Daniel proposed to me and I consented.

I wasn't even sure what it meant. "To be married" was natural, something that eventually happened to people. It wasn't a desire or a need or a goal to achieve. The victory offered excitement which was contagious, and a sense of elevation. We all felt larger than size, invincible supermen. Nothing was impossible. I said yes to Daniel because I trusted him. Because Amnon was buried and victory was won and I had no plans. I said yes because he loved me and we were friends.

I was grateful to Daniel for his calm manner. We accepted the desision and left each other alone with it to digest and accommodate.

From Jerusalem we returned to the Sinai, stopping in Tel-Aviv for an hour to call my mother and his sister and tell them we'd be married within a month. My mother reacted strangely. More hurt by not being consulted than elated by the good news.

"Do I know him?" she asked.

"Neither do I," I tried to joke. Only it wasn't a joke.

I looked at marriage as a slow trip to discovery. I expected to find new things behind turns and adjust to them, resent or love them, compromise when I had to, or fight them. I was excited by the unknown and didn't wish to prepare myself for it.

We drove south from Tel-Aviv along the coast and past the green line into the desert and night. Daniel caressed my hand occasionally or fondly touched my hair, and by the time we approached the dim lights of our camp I was fast asleep, head resting on his knee. When he woke me up, I vaguely remembered that I had made a major decision that day—changed my life, committed myself—but I didn't question it.

"I can't believe it," Beni exclaimed, hearing our news.

He had known Daniel for many years and through several wars. For a moment he gave me the impression that he thought Daniel deserved better.

"I'm not good enough for your friend," I laughed.

"Quite the contrary. I can't imagine him as a husband, but we welcome him to the club of the obedient."

I walked with Daniel for a while. Amid the charred enemy tanks and shell holes already filled with clean sand. Wounded monsters, incapacitated and dumb. Victory was exhilarating, but the destruction it caused others was nonetheless sad.

"You can still change your mind," he said, very calmly.

"So can you."

"I know you better than you'll ever know me. This may upset you. There are facts and sentiments in my past I could never share, not even look back at. You are open and inquisitive, and not having the keys to the locked door can hurt you."

"Do you love me, Daniel?"

"I love you very much. I told you so last night, and I didn't ask you the question. I'm not going to."

We left it at that and kissed under a starry moonless sky. He walked me to the tent I shared with two other girls, and I tiptoed in barefoot.

I clearly remember I dreamed of snowflakes. Snow covering the dunes and the tents. There were no clouds and the stars shone and the snow fell like manna sliding off cannon barrels and choppers' blades. I woke up to the blazing sun and the sudden morning heat. Woven into my new happiness was also a sense of resignation and acceptance. As if a cycle had closed and another one opened, trapping me comfortably.

Marriage was about friendship, compromises, security and lowering of defenses. From high-heeled shoes into slippers, and some dreams to be locked in hidden compartments, the key thrown away.

The word "forever" suddenly frightened me. The drifting would stop, I knew. There was a shore, and as beautiful as it was, it was "forever," and as wide and deep as the new ground was it was still an island surrounded by moral codes and taboos and limitations.

We were wed on a summer afternoon, the modest ceremony followed by a reception in Beni's garden. Wedding gifts—mostly pots and pans and flower vases—piled up in the bedroom and Daniel was as confused and slightly bored as I was. We held hands reassuring each other and drove to his apartment later. There was no honeymoon. Lovemaking was satisfactory, if not passionate, and we sheltered each other into self-sufficiency. In a week we had a daily routine; after a couple of months we needed very few words and communicated without them. There was work, a few friends, and later a new apartment and the first child.

The doorbell interrupted my thoughts. There was an unshaven red-eyed soldier who smiled faintly. "No alarm. Just a letter from the colonel."

He handed me an envelope.

I asked him in for coffee, but he had no time.

"Twenty-four-hour leave," he said, "so much to do," and winked. He left and I opened the letter.

"My Amalia," it read, "I don't know where to start, so I'll leave the tales to my return. I am glad I am here—less exhausted than those who have been fighting, some fresh ideas. We are going to evacuate soon, I suppose, but the Egyptians will not forget our presence here, in Africa, so near Cairo. It's primitive and beautiful, an oasis of tropical plants and waterways, flat and docile. So different from the Sinai we knew together. Beni is still superman though many of his men are dead. I miss you and the children, more than you can imagine, and think of all the things we have done together, the small things and the big ones we shall still do.

"The destruction of this war only emphasizes the need to live fully, and the routine we have created for ourselves will have to change. I doubt that this is the last war, so between now and the next one we shall have to swallow life in bigger doses. Only here do I realize what you've been through at the hospital. I'll try to call you, please take care and kiss the children. I love you. D."

The children were home, like hand-delivered birthday gifts. Runny noses and pink faces, shining eyes and half-sentences, little fingers hugging me and wet lips on my cheeks. With them there were no thoughts of the past, no dreams of the future, just joy of now and here and no time for question marks.

It was a sunny day and we packed our lunch in a basket and walked to the nearby field to look for snails, ragworts and turtles. We sat on the wet grass and our shoes were heavy with mud. We ran among

the winter flowers and invented funny names for them.
Two falcons hovered above us searching prey and a
black cloud approached from the west, above the sea,
pushing the blue away. I didn't believe in omens but it
was time to go home.

As I put the children to bed and listened to the
news, I felt strange. For weeks now I had been in the
ward at this time. The hospital quickly became a
memory, but the habit of ordinary life hadn't yet
resumed. Something was different. Not only the absence of Daniel, whose letter I read to the boys, but
the sense of security that I always felt with nightfall.
Children tucked in bed after a bath, a Bach record
in the background, the hot cup of tea and a warm
hand-knitted pullover were not sufficient. I had
doubts. Doubts about our strength, our victory, our
future, our reason.

I called Shula in the hospital. She assured me all
was calm and promised to say good-night to Avi for
me. No. 7's condition had worsened in the last hours
and Leib was in the room with him.

I said I'd come in the morning and she wished me
pleasant dreams. I seldom had dreams and I couldn't
sleep. For the first time in weeks I was in bed at
night and my eyes remained wide open. My head
felt empty, one thought chasing another and then
evaporating as I sank into a world of flimsy fantasy.

I wanted to fall in love. Not again, but differently.
I saw myself running along a beach on an exotic island,
Fiji, Jamaica, Martinique, any strange name. And
there I meet someone I know. Not a face I can identify,
and not a stranger, but someone who was, is, there
all along. We are walking in the moonlight, there

are palm trees and night birds and the sound of waves caressing billions of sand grains. We make love, we touch, we say silly things and I am filled to saturation with a heaving growing emotion until I lose control. The man is always a silhouette—wide shouldered and tall. Young but not boyish. His voice is deep and I can't see his face. The man has no face, and I, too, am only a silhouette. Lighter, legs longer than mine, hair darker, eyes greener, everything accentuated and perfected. I didn't really want it to happen. I wasn't an adventurer; I was afraid of the unknown. I would never make it alone to Martinique anyway, and missing heartbeats because of great emotions frightened me. But it was good to lie awake and imagine, then pull the blanket up, curl into its folds and sleep.

Rani coughed in his sleep. I gave him some water and watched him smile and sleep again. He wouldn't let go of my hand, and I sat there watching his curly head on the pillow. One bed with one child, not the rows of white beds in the large room in the ward. Did we always suppress the thought of another war, watching our children? It couldn't happen to us. Amnon thought so and he is gone, his son is alive but an invalid. Daniel is in the middle of mine fields and No. 7 is parentless. Rani let go of my hand and I looked at Ofer, for the first time thinking of him in uniform and feeling a pain in my chest. As if all the tears in the world formed a huge wave mounting and stopping just there, between the ribs and the throat. I didn't cry. It couldn't happen. This had to be the last war.

When I entered the ward the next morning I knew we were all losers. In daylight I saw the corners and the scars, and even the white, which at night showed clean recovery, seemed gray and stained. Behind the laughter and greetings of the boys there was a touch of defeat. Futility was stronger than victory and the sunlight pouring in exposed us all. Leib greeted me with a fatigued smile. He was leaving. Two surgeons had returned from field hospitals, and though he was asked to stay, he felt he had done his share.

I hoped he wouldn't crack the usual half-joke, "See you next war," but he did. Banality was contagious, too. He gave me a couple of novels he'd read and liked, and promised to write. We walked together to the last room. Two monitors were brought in during the night; Arik's life was a hopeless countdown now. His entire existence was horizontal lines, jumping occasionally, reaching electronic peaks and forming yellow canyons on a screen.

"That's it," Leib sighed. "A matter of hours. Makes me leave with a sense of failure, guilt perhaps."

"You saved many others."

"I never counted my gains, only the losses."

"He won't die nameless, for what it's worth."

"It makes it worse in a way. It's a definite life reaching an end, not a bundle of matter and bandages."

Leib stayed in the room staring at the screen, and I went to talk to Avi.

"Happy to present to you my daylight self," he smiled.

"My pleasure. You look awful. Had a good night?"

He was well enough to flirt and there was nothing brotherly in the way he held my hand.

"The sun becomes you," he stated. "You should

change your hairdo and get out of uniform and you could be quite smashing."

"Thanks. We are friends, remember?"

"My sister is blushing. I'm a few years late, but you should give me a second chance."

Did he remember? A thousand years ago he gave me a ride home on his bicycle. When we were near the garden gate he suggested we share a cigarette. We were teenagers. I was plump and unhappy with my looks and his pimples hid among the freckles. It was spring and the smell of the cheap cigarette mixed with the purest of orange blossom odor. He said he didn't really like the brother-sister theme we played. He touched my hand which held his bike and said in all seriousness, "You attract me sexually." I didn't laugh then. I didn't answer or move, as if his words in themselves meant doing something wrong or premature. There were girls who "gave" and others who didn't, like myself. He thought my silence meant consent and his thin fine hand moved hesitantly to the brassiere's hook. There was a light in my parents' bedroom window and I managed to say, "Not here."

"Let's go somewhere then."

"Why do something we shall regret?"

Once I regained my speech he let go, and we discussed it in length. Talking things over was as intimate then as doing them. We shared a secret. He thought love followed the touching of breasts and I said it should precede it. In a clownish gesture he kissed the top of my head, promised to try again, and I entered the house feeling very womanly.

It never happened again, we never talked about it, and I never before remembered the scene.

Now he was a war casualty, a volunteer from the States, Julie's estranged husband and the father of Karen. I was Daniel's wife and mother of two and though not for a second did I wish to encourage him, I felt a sense of warmth at the thought of being wanted, as casual as it was.

My recollections of the next hour are vague. Nadav wheeled himself in, proud of the progress he was making. I saw the bent figure of Professor Rothman hurrying along the corridor, past the open door. There was commotion at the far end of the ward. The day nurses followed the Professor, returned, passed again. I must have felt that whatever was happening needed professional attention so I stayed glued to the chair clutching Avi's hand.

Avi summoned Leib when he caught sight of him. The doctor said to him in English, "He died. The guy in the last room."

"Arik," I said. "That was his name. Arik Berkov."

They must have disconnected the tubes, electrodes, needles in minutes for before long, still sitting there unable to move, I saw the nurse pushing the bed out. It hit the wall and mechanically I said, "Watch out." I couldn't see the corpse. A sheet covered the bandaged head. We never knew him really alive.

I must have fainted when the bed was transferred. I remember circles, gray and white, growing wider, then narrowing, and a strong nausea.

When I came to, I was in the Professor's room, a cold towel on my forehead and a strong smell of valerian in my nostrils.

I tried to sit and couldn't and mumbled words of

apology. Leib tried to talk to me and, suddenly aggressive, I hushed him.

The nurse said she had called my mother and she was home with the children. I couldn't drive, and one of the interns would take me home.

The Professor asked to be left alone with me.

"I know you cared. You refused to accept the void. For us it didn't matter. A life saved, fought for, has a biological identity, even if relatives don't surround the bed. To us he had identity just as much as the next patient."

"I know you tried."

"You had an accusing look at times. As if we were letting him die, as if he were an object to us. It wasn't true."

"My head feels heavy."

"Gideon will take you home. Better take a few days off. We are slowly returning to normal. You're always welcome as a visitor."

No, he didn't say we shall meet in the next war. He, too, felt he had had his share and managed to think about it as the last one.

A doctor called Gideon drove me home. I asked him to tell Avi I'd call him. He helped me to the apartment, stroked the heads of the children, and explained to my mother that I needed rest.

"Accumulation, you know. It happens to all of us. A spring unwinding. I just returned to the ward today. A patient died, perhaps someone she was attached to."

He left. I closed the bedroom door and lay on the bed in my uniform. I shivered and felt an enormous wave mount up from my chest, choking and heaving, and the tears were streaming.

I, too, was a loser. Not a victim, not a sacrifice, just a plain loser. I clung to margins, held to edges and sought security in outskirts, corners. Now I was thrown in and helpless, pathetic in my inability to cope without even the comfort of self-pity.

Daniel, I whispered. I wanted him. How I needed him now. His words, his touch, his silence.

Yes, I talked to him. We will swallow life hungrily. We shall do things never done, dream and fulfill, and there on the beach in Jamaica my lover's silhouette suddenly had a face and it was Daniel's. We shall reach the sky and the horizon and fly together and love. "Oh, please," I whispered, "come back soon."

BOOK TWO

Daniel

I left Amalia a short note, packed a few things and changed. The khaki uniform was too clean, too starched, too well ironed. The war was almost over and I felt like a toy soldier walking down the stairs of the apartment house. It was foolish to leave, but impossible to stay: Beni had insisted he could use me.

I drove past the outskirts of Tel-Aviv and along the shore road heading south. When the orange groves were behind me and the first sand dunes appeared pale yellow and wet, I felt better. The green fields, the forests and the hills covered with flowers I associated with picnics and the children. The bare desert, cracked land, treeless landscape was man's land. Men behind camels or driving jeeps or inside tanks. Men exposed to each other—as enemies or friends. I stopped near Gaza for some soldiers returning to their units from a short leave. They fell asleep as I turned west into the Sinai. Refidim, the large dusty camp in the center of Sinai, was as far as I could go in my own car. Last time it was with Amalia's head in my lap, sleeping while I caressed her hair. A day earlier I had proposed to her and I still wondered whether it was instinctive or the result of thought. It didn't matter. I was committed and had no regrets. There was something compact about her, earthy without being vulgar, strong without the need to prove it. Perhaps for the first time I had met a woman who was free of the feminine paraphernalia, the games, the caprices, the makeup inside and outside. There were no tears, no exclamation marks, no coyness, no miniature tragedies, no pretence of dependence. No feminine mystery either, just the profound mystery of another human being, another complex of brain and heart to be explored and shared. There was no vanity, only self-esteem, knowledge of what was there and what was lacking, no perfection.

For six years we've been together, sharing growing pains and rounding the edges. The Amalia I left today is the same person I married six years ago. No subdued looks of a domesticated female, no added glamor in order to fight fleeting time, the same earnestness I took with a smile, the efficiency I marveled at, the attempt at being an outsider, failing so often. Never since we met did I want another woman. I almost regretted the affairs I had had before. The futility and waste of time of the short flimsy relationships. The crudeness and simplicity of brief emotional involvements, the poverty and dullness of communication I had had with other women, were stains on my memory, without pleasure or joy or pride.

For a moment I felt terrible about leaving the way I did. A coward. I had left a note as if Amalia were my landlady. I already missed the children, was afraid to think of them, as a physical pain surged in my chest whenever I did. I had a job to do, back in action. I was well equipped for it and I had no regrets, only I wish they could have been here with me, the three of them, in the back seat rather than in my mind. In the back seat the soldiers were asleep. Amalia was at the hospital or asleep at home, my children were safe and innocent and I was heading south, naturally, willingly, but with a heavy heart.

I parked the car next to other civilian vehicles, woke up my passengers and locked the doors. From Headquarters I called Beni. He suggested I spend the night in Refidim, and drive out the next morning with one of his unit's doctors who was expected in the field hospital that night.

The girl-soldier in the communication center offered me coffee. It was too sweet but it was hot and I needed it.

"They are fighting up north," she said. That was all.

"Have you been here all along?" She was a plump girl, brown hair gathered back and smooth skinned. Her eyes expressed sympathy without mischief.

"No. When the war started I was near the canal. We were evacuated to Beer-Sheba and returned here a few days ago. Are you back from home leave? I haven't seen you before."

"A six-year home leave. No. I'm joining Beni now. I left Refidim after the '67 war. It's changed."

"It's a city now. Do you like music?"

I didn't answer. The question didn't register.

"There is a chamber-music concert tonight."

I left my bag with her. My name was written on the canvas with a felt pen.

"Daniel Darom," she read. "I am Dina. See you later."

I walked out, and buttoned my wind jacket. It wasn't the desert camp I knew. The boots didn't sink in the sand and the sky was overcast, then dark, without a sunset. Blackout was observed, and the headlights of vehicles coming and going were painted dark blue. I looked for the familiar—a face, a landscape, our old headquarters. I had memories. I was there, where things had happened to me, and I felt like a stranger surrounded by children. Young boys in uniform, well protected from the wind, hurried by. Nobody asked me who I was or what I wanted there. It felt like a foreign city where they were speaking a strange language or another planet. I followed the sound of a helicopter landing and arrived at the airstrip. The skeletons of Russian choppers were still there, leftovers from 1967, but unapproachable. Three helicopters landed, one after the other, and people hurried toward them. They were unloaded and reloaded and took off. And silence again. I thought of going to the field hospital to look for Beni's doctor, then changed my mind and looked for the officers' dining room.

There was a concert tonight, Dina had said. Chamber music. For another hour I wandered about. It felt rather good not to know anybody. The war machine was operating; people did what they had to do. It wasn't the endless chatter around a bonfire, no longer the small familiar group of people one has met before and is bound to meet again. It was a responsible and well-organized center delegating orders, sending supplies, taking in casualties, communicating with divisions and regiments miles away. Somewhere this machine had a heart, warmth, human feeling.

In the hoarse voice of commanders, the care with which the stretchers were handled, even the way the girls handled the paperwork late into the night.

I followed a couple of pilots and found myself in front of the guarded war room.

The guard looked at my papers. Someone was summoned, and I said I wanted to report. I was invited to enter, offered cake and a sandwich and a young captain for company.

The general was away. His deputy should be in soon, and I was welcome to one of the spare beds in the war room, he said. He called the hospital and located the doctor who was to pick me up at dawn to drive to Beni's division. The war room was busy. Many low voices can still form a noisy atmosphere; most of the people around talked incessantly. I recognized a couple of journalists, a writer, and two colonels I had known as majors.

I walked back to Dina's bunker for my bag. She wasn't there; another girl smiled at me and gave me my things. I returned to the war room and stretched out on a bed in the dimly lit corner.

A visitor, that's what I was. I was visiting the outskirts of war.

Still it was better than home. The illusion of participation, the comfort of solitude.

Ofer and Rani are asleep, I thought. My mother-in-law is reading, my wife is "doing her share" in the hospital. Our bed in empty.

Was it here in Refidim that I decided to marry Amalia?

Six years ago this place was a fly-ridden post in the desert. I was lonely and even jealous of my friends who talked about their wives and children. I truly thought that if there were to be another war, I, too, would like to have someone to go back to. Now I ran away from it. Not because I resented it, or found it unsatisfactory, but because it was the right place to long for, the wrong place to be in.

The captain brought me a couple of blankets.

"I am on duty tonight, you can use mine. You know where the coffee and sandwiches are. I'll wake you up at four-thirty."

When the captain touched my shoulder in the morning, I woke up and smiled at him. As if this were my routine. As if for weeks now I had slept on this iron bed under army blankets in the war room. I used my battery-powered razor and washed my face, put on the boots, and enjoyed the coffee and crackers.

"Your transportation is outside," someone said.

"Thanks for the hospitality."

"Good trip."

I was given some mail to take to Beni. It was still dark outside and very cold. The doctor was a man my age, slightly bald and shortsighted. He introduced himself, Yaron, and we shook hands. He pulled a woolen cap over his head and ears and offered me the front seat in the jeep. I chose to sit behind, put a blanket on my knees and held on to the machine-gun butt to my right and the wireless set on my left.

We left the camp and headed west toward the canal. With daylight I noticed we weren't alone on the road. Two half-tracks with soldiers were in front and a supply lorry in back of us. It was foggy and dusty and the doctor kept cleaning his eyeglasses.

"I am a reservist, too," he volunteered.

"What hospital?"

He used the civilian name for the central military hospital.

"My wife works there as a volunteer."

His face brightened. He was very proud of the hospital.

"She does night duty in the burns ward."

"Rothman's department. The best in the country. I am in pediatrics." He followed with a few banalities. "All sick people are children, regardless of age. I'm spared the jokes the dentists and gynecologists get."

I looked at his hands, imagined him patting Rani's buttocks, rubbing Ofer's chest. He seemed utterly at ease here. He must have handled hundreds of serious wounds, seen corpses, disfigured limbs, torn insides, burnt flesh, yet he didn't have the haunted suffering look about him. We drove through an immense battlefield, past hundreds of torn vehicles and burnt tanks; he didn't comment on the futility or destruction or horrors of war.

"Fantastic field hospital in Refidim," he said with pride again. "I'm glad I am with Beni, though. Not being a surgeon, and working with excellent young doctors, I feel I am more of use."

He used superlatives all along. Everything was "fantastic," "excellent" or merely "great." The soldiers, the African scenery where Beni camped, even the food.

"You've got a good defense mechanism," I said needlessly.

The jeep halted and then pulled to the right. Two tank carriers were trying to pass us on the left. The driver of the first one shouted at us, something about the Hermon. It must have been good news, for he was smiling and turning his thumb up.

"Bullshit," Yaron spat as the jeep moved again.

I wasn't sure whether this was meant as an answer to my comment or a reaction to the cloud of dust that engulfed us.

He was right, of course. My own eyes did not reflect the profound sadness I expected to find in his. I felt that way during the first day of the last war. I looked at the pathetic Egyptians—dead or injured or taken prisoners. I felt compassion, I felt guilty, as if a chunk of my humanity had been removed. A few hours later we were under fire and our first casualties were evacuated. My terms of reference changed, and I talked, thought, felt the language of war—I had to destroy or be destroyed and that was that. It had nothing to do with "defense mechanism."

We were moving very slowly now, and at the intersection before crossing the canal we stopped altogether. On the road parallel to the canal, going north, a long convoy was blocking traffic. We were given an hour to wait our turn to go west and joined a platoon sitting in the ditch preparing a late breakfast.

They were opening sardine cans and serving more crackers, plum jam and hot tea. All the tastes and memories of the last war came back to me. One thing was missing—the smell—the dreadful nauseating stench of human flesh rotting in the June sun was missing. It was warm and clear, but the dominant smell was that of fuel and fumes and smoke.

Three jets dived low above us. Ours. They headed west and left beautiful white trails behind. How I envied them. Faster than sound, reflecting the sun and mastering the airspace, manipulating the sophisticated weapon systems and artfully maneuvering between altitudes toward the missile sites near Ismailia and Suez. I envied their precision and elegance. It was absurd. I was good at other things, very good in fact. I had dealt with intricate matters in the past and displayed imagination, courage, initiative, and here I sat in a ditch, waiting for a heavy convoy to clear the way, and wanting to fly.

My frustrations, flying and medicine. The jets disappeared, diving low, and Dr. Yaron was munching a cracker next to me. Medicine I never even tackled, just coveted, and flying school I flunked. "Unfit to be a pilot," they said. I hadn't tried hard enough. I took my ability and talent for granted, and I didn't make it.

"What day is today?" the doctor asked.

"Tuesday, I suppose. The twenty-third."

"Thanks. I thought so. It's somebody's birthday—my wife's? My daughter's? I am hopeless about dates."

It was very hot now. We took off our jackets and rolled up our shirt-sleeves. We were slowly nearing the bridge among hundreds of damaged vehicles, some still smoking. We could hear the artillery from the other side of the canal. The cease-fire was fiction, the war was still on. More planes flew over us, crossing the canal above us and splitting—some to the north, others south along the western coast of the Great Bitter Lake. I could see the bridge now. Rafts attached to each other, each sinking with the weight of the vehicle crossing, and refloating to receive the next one.

"There are three bridges now," Yaron volunteered. "I crossed first in a rubber boat, under fire, and I am a lousy swimmer. It feels better now." The lorry in front was crossing now, and we followed. Soon we were on the other side, leaving behind us the canal, the Sinai, Asia, the desert, into the fertile cultivated strip, an agricultural barrier separating two deserts flourishing on a sweet-water canal and human manure.

Soon our little convoy of five cars separated from the others and turned north on the road to Ismailia.

"So, isn't it fantastic?" Yaron insisted.

He was referring to the vegetation. Along the road two streams of sweet-water sent healthy liquid fingers to small squares of cultivated patches. The palm trees were majestic, crowned with ripe dates, and green vegetables were neatly lined in garden beds.

The mud huts were deserted, and a few platoons of infantry soldiers walked among them or camped among the orange trees. It was a treacherous area. Visibility was limited to a few meters, empty Egyptian barracks and storehouses offered shelter to enemy snipers, if they chose not to run away. The exposure of the desert was gone, and this oasis offered anything but security. I held the machine gun as we advanced, and the doctor pulled a submachine gun from under his seat and made sure it was loaded.

We camped in the dunes, just west of this fertile stinking paradise. Another five miles altogether. My ears grew accustomed to the sound of bombs falling somewhere and the sporadic bursts of machine-gun fire. Troops were advancing north and south of us, using the time that was left until a real cease-fire would be declared and implemented.

"You bring us luck," the driver said. "It's the first time I took the bridge without having to jump for shelter before or after. They must be running short on shells."

Yaron hushed him. He wasn't superstitious, he said, but don't count your luck or your blessings before you are safely back home.

"Do you have children?" he asked me, as if this were the only piece of information lacking in his knowledge of me.

"Two small boys."

We kept watching the roadside as we advanced and took a left turn on a dirt road, crossing a small bridge over a narrow canal. The road was bumpy and short and a few hundred yards in front of us I could see the familiar silhouette of Beni's trailer, painted green and brown.

CHAPTER 10

Beni must have been in conference for I could hear voices as I climbed up the metal ladder and opened the door.

On the long table which occupied most of the trailer there were three large maps and a helmet full of dates. Beni was at the head of the table, his back to me. I lightly touched his shoulder, and he rose and turned. We embraced warmly, and he pointed to the bench along the wall.

"You know everybody? My brigade commanders— Gidi, Aaron and Johnny. Have some dates and coffee and listen in. Undivided attention you'll get in fifteen minutes."

I sat on the shabby upholstered bench. Beni lit his pipe and listened carefully to what his men had to say. His red eyes disclosed sleepless nights and fatigue, but the boyish luster was there. He was in a good mood. The horrors behind, he had a cleaning-up job to do. Missile sites in his sector were all destroyed and his troops controlled the Cairo-Ismailia road and railway. That meant no more casualties, full air support in case of action, and time enough for the forces to rest and reorganize. The commanders around the

table were less relaxed. They were younger and their
eyes reflected the casualties their brigades suffered.
They didn't believe in the declared cease-fire and
wanted reinforcement and more ammunition.

"I've talked to Arik," Beni snapped. "The southern
division has blocked the two Suez-Cairo roads and
may go into the city of Suez within forty-eight hours
if the cease-fire isn't valid."

"Are we going into Ismailia?" Alon asked.

"No. The sewage plant is where we stop in the
north. Very poetic. Just give your men a rest, good
food and clean water. Send patrols to the plantations
and mud huts, make sure the area is clean and secure.
Anything else?"

There was silence and the men got up, folding their
maps. Gidi stayed a minute to discuss a personal
problem. When he left I was alone with Beni.

"Good kids," he said. "You saw the bridgehead.
You know what they've been through."

"It's good to be here," I said. "Should have come
earlier."

"You had no business here earlier, but since Gideon
was wounded, I missed you. The kids are fine, but
each of us needs one or two old-timers around for the
small hours and the tough moments. What we share
we'll never have in common with the young ones."

We talked a brief moment about wives and children.

"I wish my wife had hospital duty or something," he
said. "It took me years to convince her that generals
don't get hurt in battle. Well, it didn't quite work this
time."

"Amalia knows I'm here. She doesn't know what for.

In case she calls—I'm helping you on postwar logistics."

"Do you want to talk business now? What are the proposed dates anyway? I was about to go for a drive, show you my kingdom."

"Two alternatives. Wednesday the 24th or Thursday the 25th. We should plan for both. I presume you are the only one who knows about 'The Phoenix'?"

"Some Phoenix. Nobody knows, and I wish I didn't either. Gideon is on the critical list, otherwise I wouldn't send you in his footsteps. However important this man is I'd hate to see you risk your life, and I don't care very much for his."

"Gideon shouldn't have looked for him in the bridgehead area."

"And didn't I tell him? What kind of planning is it, anyway? To try to rescue an agent from the most heavily bombarded spot in the area? But he insisted, as if it were his first-born. In case he makes it there, he said. So he got it, and two others did, too, and your Phoenix was probably sipping mango juice in Cairo or Campari in Rome. Only twelve hours later did they let us know that another time and place had been proposed. Trust the service. They should have sent one of their own well-trained heroes to the bridgehead just after the crossing."

"Gideon was one of their well-trained men. So am I, I suppose." Beni continued, "Gideon joined me to fight a war. He would have come with or without exotic birds for an excuse. So would you, perhaps, if you could. Or am I counting on a friendship that has only professional depth?"

"Oh, cut it!"

I didn't really want to get into an argument. He loved Gideon. He felt responsible. He couldn't tolerate the thought that he may have lost him for some unknown, unsuccessful agent. Woven into his bitterness was the fact that our world-famous service did not foresee the war, did not forecast the crossing of the canal, the use of individual missiles, the size of the forces the Egyptians had put into this battle. As far as he was concerned, the service didn't justify their reputation, or indeed their existence.

"He isn't a bad fellow," was all I could say, "and he may have some vital information on him, even if this is the end of the war."

"Vital information is sixteen days late. As for his being a good or bad guy, I don't want to know. You told me stories, didn't you? Here, in this trailer, across the Sinai in 1967, about freaks, rejects, half-castes, people you had a hold on. Men who worked for money, others who did the double game. One out of ten was a genuine patriotic hero, and nine were miserable liars or pathetic failures.

"Phoenix can't go back to Cairo. He's done a job. He has to be found and sent into Israel. Why are we arguing? There is no more danger involved than in any other rescue operation during the war."

"OK. Don't tell me more or I'll feel sorry for the bastard. Here is the map of the area, let's work it out and I'll ask the cook to prepare us the best dinner west of the Suez."

Beni walked out to look for the cook and I sat there staring at the map. My mind felt rusty. I was tired, and questions rather than answers crowded the air between me and the map. The new date was set in accordance with the expected cease-fire. The office had not communicated with Phoenix since the war had started, and figured it should be easier for him to arrive at our front post while both armies were resting and reorganizing. He had cover-papers. He was a foreigner, and his job as a hydraulic engineer justified his presence in the canal area. He had rented a small villa north of Suez, and the fictitious company had an office in this town.

Beni returned with news of the menu and many question marks.

"Why hasn't he communicated since the war started? Isn't that when they are really called upon to display courage, sophistication, initiative?"

I wished I knew. So many things could have gone wrong. The whole canal area was under fire. Regular communications were cut off and as far as I knew he may have been hiding for days now, lying low waiting for a chance to join our forces. Gideon had looked for him in the bridgehead area on a hunch. A wrong one. If he had important information on him, certainly he'd hold it until we got to him.

Beni made it clear that his units were not involved in the planning to take over Suez. I was using his experience and imagination, but the details would have to be worked out with the southern division commander.

"You don't have to go there before tomorrow afternoon. By then we'll know whether the operation is on. I can spare a jeep and a couple of people to accompany you, so you will be independent. But all other facilities I can't guarantee. Nor take the responsibility," he added with emphasis.

He pushed the map out of the way.

"The rest after dinner," he said, and poured us both a fair measure of cognac from a flask.

"*L'chaim*. Good to have you here."

An officer came in with a large envelope addressed to me. Inside it was an unaddressed envelope, and in the third one there was a photocopy of a few numbered pages, each marked "Top Secret." There was also a photograph of Phoenix.

"Pinups from the office," I said. "Better take a look in case something happens to me and you have to identify the fellow."

"Quite careless of them, isn't it? In spite of the clever packaging."

"Urgency precedes caution, I suppose. Look, register and destroy—as they used to tell me."

"A regular film star," he commented, holding the glossy photo. Phoenix was good-looking, in an ordinary, somehow effeminate way. He was fair, with dark brown eyes—one slightly smaller than the other. His lips were thin above a square determined chin. In the photo he sported a tweed jacket, striped tie and a matching kerchief in the jacket pocket.

"Very British, indeed," Beni summed up. "Very inconspicuous in this area, just blending in with the retreating Egyptians or the advancing Israelis. You think he is alive and having his tea in a Suez cafe, do you? Or is he clad in a djellaba and riding a camel?" He tore up the picture and threw the bits away.

The cook came in with a tray and I had to admit that, east or west of Suez, this was a good meal. When the dishes were removed and the map placed once again on the folding wooden table, we both assumed a professional look and discussed the operation. We disagreed from the beginning. Beni thought I should follow the armor and infantry, stay a safe distance behind and go into the area when it was ours.

"If he is hiding," he said, "and has managed so far, he can stick it out another couple of days. No need to take risks. If the cease-fire is implemented and the city is in our hands, the 3rd Army cut off and surrounded, you can take your time, walk the streets, knock politely on doors, ask questions—get to the man and fly him back to Tel-Aviv, stopping here for coffee."

I knew it couldn't be done that way. I had to search for him in the confusion of the battle. If he had survived so far, we couldn't have him killed "by mistake" by our infantry, or blown to pieces by an air bomb or artillery shell. I also doubted that we would be able to complete occupation of a city as large as Suez. Cease-fire might be declared just as the battle is on, and I might miss him by two street corners or one hour.

We settled for somewhere in between. I was to follow the first wave of attack. I was not to cross into a sector which was not fully in our hands, but I would try to achieve it all before cease-fire was finally declared and observed.

"Just limit yourself to two places," he actually ordered. "If he isn't in the villa or the office, you let go. Get into the jeep and return here for supper. Is that a deal?"

He had to make a few calls, and I walked out for some air. The sky was bright but not as starry as I had imagined. Occasionally I could hear gusts of small gun fire.

It was another world. Unfamiliar, unlike deserts we knew, and not half as exotic as Beni tried to make it. The lack of contact with Phoenix did disturb me. He was a fastidious operator, handy with all electronic devices and very professional. There were many possible explanations—he could have been wounded, even hospitalized. He may have saved his skin and gone into hiding, without any equipment. He may be doing his job fervently, gathering information and trusting we'd come for him. He could be dead, too. But as long as there was no proof of that, it was our duty to try. Obviously, he had failed at some point. The Egyptian attack was a total surprise, and if he were there, on the spot, and noticed nothing, it was an unforgivable failure—unless he was sure we knew what to him seemed so obvious from the other side.

Whatever, I figured, I have to give it a try. The good old sense of responsibility settled comfortably in. Like in Europe ten years ago. I was responsible whether I liked the agents or not, whether they delivered or not.

When I returned to the trailer, Beni was still on the phone. It occurred to me that it had been only one day since I left home, that I hadn't thought of the children since the day I left them. That was entirely schizophrenic. Here, in the field, on the eve of an operation, I functioned and operated as a single man. As if the years in between had never happened. I had to apply my brain and memory, with an effort, to reconstruct our bedroom. Where was the telephone at home? What shirt did I wear yesterday? The children from this distance seemed smaller than they actually were.

Small heads, fine features, static slides without sound rather than a lively presence.

"Wouldn't you like to call Amalia?" Beni suggested, as if he could read her name in my expression.

"It's too late. I'll call tomorrow. If she calls here when I am away, find an excuse and tell her I'll call back."

"I call my wife daily. The one day I didn't manage, she was already mourning me. Tears, sedation and all. Is it that bad up there? They never had to wait so long."

"It's nervousness. Frustration and incredibility. The first few days we were told—the public was told—we were winning. In minds and hearts it was a repetition of 1967. Then the truth came out and people refused to believe. All the trust and confidence disappeared. The well-being of years fell apart and the supermen dream shattered. Then rumors of the number of casualties, no contact with the front and no possible end."

"And when we began advancing? When we crossed the canal?"

"People didn't know what to believe anymore. The loss was heavier than the gain. The loss was measured by lives, the gain—square miles."

I continued, "I don't think you know Rudi, he lives in Ramat-Gan. His son was killed in the Chinese Farm Battle, I went to see him. We served together in London and he returned a year ago after a long absence.

"It was his only son. He was sitting on the sofa in his small apartment, hugging his wife and crying. He didn't register my entrance, but when I was about to leave he grabbed me. He threw at me all the accusations possible. The politicians who didn't lead, the generals who didn't plan, the service that didn't warn, the illusions we padded our nest with until we were smothered into blindness. There was nothing I could say. He was right and he was entirely wrong. A man in pain doesn't have to be sensible anyway. I left him and went to see my boss in the service. I wanted him to go and visit Rudi, talk to him, help him get rid of his bitterness.

"Before I managed to talk he told me Gideon was wounded, asked me to take over this operation. I mentioned Rudi to him, told him what state he was in. You know what he said? 'I can't face these things.'"

"'These things,' those were the words he used! My boss, too, has a son fighting the Syrians somewhere. Defense mechanism? So I went home and left Amalia a note and here I am. You did ask how were things away from the battlefield . . ."

I wasn't sure whether Beni was still with me. He was facing me but his eyes seemed to stare at something beyond.

"What time should I leave for David's Headquarters?"

"We'll decide tomorrow. They are dug in, and if there is still exchange of artillery fire, we'll have to find the right moment. Do you know how many families I have to visit when I return? How many mothers and wives I have to see? Do you know how it scares me?"

"It does help them."

"Like another marble on the tomb. Not that they blame me. They know I've exposed myself, never far away from danger. The first visit I manage. We sit and I tell them about the battle in which they lost their son or father or husband. The children are brought in and I shake their hands and pat their heads. Then the second visit, and the tenth and a dozen more and I feel the whole world is composed of orphans and widows and tears and sighs. I feel I represent everything they will hate forever. The uniform, the red beret, my dusty boots, my trite remarks about sacrifice and devotion. I feel like a rotten jukebox—feed it a bereaved family and it produces a neat little speech."

We were both tired. He was at the end of a battle, I was facing one, we both needed rest and time alone. He walked with me to the tent next to the trailer. I was issued field uniform, a new helmet and submachine gun.

"I have no identity discs," I mentioned.

"Do you have an officers' identity card?"

This I did have, and we left it at that. I was given a sleeping bag and a blanket for the night and said good-night to Beni who climbed back to the trailer.

I chose the soft patch next to a half-track and got into the sleeping bag. I didn't like tents, I didn't like underground shelters. I felt safest in the open air. In spite of long training at sleeping anytime, anywhere, I couldn't fall asleep. Vague thundering sounds from the south indicated a sporadic exchange of fire. Someone was making sure every fifteen minutes or so that their presence was noticed.

Amalia should be home now. My mother-in-law, whom I trusted but didn't like, was back in her apartment. Rani and Ofer would be fast asleep. Will they remember this war? I felt strange, as if something had been damaged in my system. The ability to be alone and enjoy solitude was still there, but not without an effort. I was a part of a family; I wasn't a young man anymore. I wasn't as comfortable in the sleeping bag as I used to be, and there was something sterile in the taste of danger which used to excite me. I didn't miss the slippers and the late night talk with Amalia, or the home cooking or the children's presence. I was only two days away from home. It wasn't that what I left I longed for, it was that what I found was not the way I remembered it. Priorities had changed. I wasn't anxious to get into a battle, take risks, run like a fool seeking shelter under fire or crossing a minefield. I had a home, I had responsibilities—by choice, by love. The front-line sense of freedom I must have lost forever. My thoughts drifted in small whirlpools rather than from a continuous line. A sense of guilt about my father surged and filled me. I had never been patient with him. He had made the big decision, which formed and determined my own life—to immigrate to Israel from Poland in the thirties —and this remained the only bond between us. Since then he had always chosen wrong. He had tried a kibbutz, then a cooperative, ended a failure in business and died a bitter, grumbling, penniless merchant. He left Poland to give his family a new life, with new dimensions, and resumed here, after twenty years of complaining, the life he had chosen to leave—a servile life, dependent on money lenders and careless partners and customers. I avoided him when I became independent. I refused to believe he could be changed, and when my mother died, I stopped seeing him altogether. He had no dreams, no aspirations, no faith. I owed him the fact that I was born here. Had he chosen otherwise, I would have been a child in Dachau, but I had a happy childhood in a kibbutz in the Galilee, while cousins of mine, never met or heard from, were shipped in cattle trains to gas chambers.

This debt made me feel guilty. Only when my own sons were born did I understand it, and it was too late to make up for it. It didn't matter much. I wasn't tormented by it, not even upset. Why I should think of him now, here in Africa, God only knows.

I must have slept a few hours. As I woke up the sun was breaking through a cloud of wet mist in the east. I joined Beni who had just gotten up, and we listened together to the sound of heavy guns firing in the distance.

"Some cease-fire," he snapped.

"I hope we are taking advantage of it."

"Just line-straightening. I am told to stay put, but when you drive south you'll run into convoys of re-inforcement. There are three bridges now and they are all jammed with everything from water-tankers to ammunition trucks and journalists in buses."

"When am I leaving?"

"Whenever you are ready. Gabi, a captain, will escort you to David. Make sure you keep your helmet on and don't get off the road. It may be a long drive."

We had a cup of coffee together. Beni was busy on the phone receiving and giving orders. It was only five in the morning, but there was a feeling of urgency, as if everything had to be done quickly before the morning and the war were really over.

Gabi arrived with a radio jeep. I sat next to him and waved to Beni. He didn't wave back, just mumbled something inaudible, and we drove east in the direction of the Great Bitter Lake.

For four hours we drove through the bridgehead. The jeep moved expertly among scores of tanks labeled "Cairo Express," trucks, tankers, buses and half-tracks. We eagerly watched three dogfights between Migs and Israeli Mirages—the Migs always ending in a spiral descent and an explosion. A dozen times we sought shelter in ditches when Egyptian gunners were aiming at the convoy. The ground around us had been smashed and furrowed by shells, and bloated corpses lay sprawled next to charred vehicles and incinerated tanks. The pressure of the helmet protecting my head and the smell of death made me slightly dizzy. But the creeping sense of having gone through all this before relaxed me.

The tanks speeded up between bursts of fire. Clouds of dust made it impossible to see. An occasional palm tree seemed entirely out of place. We were real, the white smoke and the planes were real. The sweet-water canal, the pathetic patches of cultivated land, the ruined mud shacks looked like a theatrical decor.

Gabi concentrated on the road. The shells were of no interest to him. The problem was to survive the traffic, and I was sure he was cursing me every inch of the way.

By lunch time we were south of the main Suez road and on a hill overlooking an active battlefield. We found David holding a can of peeled grapefruit sections and looking through a pair of binoculars.

I couldn't help smiling. The scene was far better

than all the stories I had heard about David—and
there were many stories. He was tall and his long
limbs seemed to interwind peculiarly. His shoelaces
were undone, but he was clean-shaven and must have
used an after-shave lotion amply. He had an ugly
face, features put together by a joker—long nose,
small eyes close together, thick lips and square chin.
He was famous for his calm in battle, for his use of
dirty language in the softest of voices. He was also
famous for his courage, his women, his extravagances.

He looked at us, acknowledged Gabi's presence and
addressed me. "You must be the master spy."

"Daniel Darom," I said and we shook hands.

"Sit down, son," he said. This I learned later was
a compliment, for he addressed most reservists as
"daddy." "Son" was reserved for soldiers and friends.

Thus adopted, I crouched next to him and was
introduced to the other officers. Gabi turned to leave.
I gave him a letter I wrote to Amalia which he promised to give to a pilot in Faid airport on his way.

"Have some grapefruit sections," David offered.

"No, thanks."

"Easy guest, ah? Hospitality I'll shower you with
later. Right now we can't even talk spy business. Not
until we screw Ras-Adabiyah. See them running, son?"

I didn't see anybody or anything. On David's map,
immaculately clean under plastic in spite of the endless number of grapefruit sections and sardines eaten
over it, I saw Adabiyah. It was south of the city of
Suez on the gulf.

"You didn't go through Suez yet?" There must have
been a trace of panic in my voice.

"Don't worry, son. What's for the service, we leave

to you. No, that's tomorrow, if Kissinger and Golda and Sadat will allow us, if the U.N. doesn't stop us, and if the weather is good—which I promise you it will be."

He had earphones attached to his helmet and his gray hair could barely be seen. He talked every few seconds to a small microphone extending from his helmet, but his expression was the same when he was talking to us and to tank commanders trotting south to capture the next point.

So when he said, "Screw the bitches," pausing between the words and taking his time to pronounce each, we weren't sure who he was talking to.

There was something exhilarating in the atmosphere. A slow sun was setting behind us, beyond Cairo and the Nile, and David emanated confidence which spread to each of us, comforting and soothing.

He must have lost half his brigade in the battles so far. The casualties were replaced, and he kept asking for the names of the new voices he was talking to. As if he were at a cocktail party—"And what did you say your name was, son?"

Suddenly he got up, hovering above us on his long legs and stretching his arms. "Fucking dunes," he said. "Let's get out of here, children."

He fitted his limbs into the front seat of a jeep, while we climbed on a half-track and followed him. One of the officers explained to me that we were returning to the provisory camp on the Suez-Cairo road. Judging by the sounds, the battle was nearing an end. The shelling became sporadic, though it never stopped, and as it grew darker we reached a well-fortified Egyptian camp where David's Headquarters was situated. A low tent served as a war room. Other than a few intelligence officers near the maps and a well-equipped communication center, the war room was quiet. Two journalists were hectically writing reports next to a wooden table, while a gentle steam rose from a tea kettle on the field gas stove.

David excused himself and disappeared, and I used the water tanker outside to remove a thick layer of dust from my face and hands.

I didn't feel tired, I didn't feel out of place, I didn't want to be anywhere else. It was a kind of home. Not busy with people one didn't know like division Headquarters. Just doing a job, doing it well and projecting a sense of professional pride and efficency.

I thought of Amalia, of myself telling Amalia about it. I wondered whether she, too, like so many women one heard of, would find David irresistible.

There was a message for me from Beni. I got him on the line.

"You got out in time," he said. "We were shelled occasionally, and spent a lousy day figuring out where the next bazooka projectile was going to hit. What's with you?"

"I feel great. David's men got to Adabiyah and the outskirts of Suez. The fertilizing plant or something. What's with the cease-fire?"

"Keep your fingers crossed. It seems we claim they broke it and we are fighting back. I doubt if it'll be effective before sometime tomorrow."

"The 3rd Army is surrounded entirely." I gave him information he must have had already. "Soon they'll ask for food and water. It's good to feel on top of it again."

"How is David treating you?"

"Like his own son."

"You too . . . Take care. We'll talk tomorrow."

David returned with a fresh can of grapefruit sections. "The fucking cook," he said, "has got a stomachache. How do you like that! To be accurate—he's got diarrhea. Doesn't that boost your appetite!"

He sent one of the junior officers to take care of the kitchen. "Before he dies, ask the cook for the soup recipe and get someone to prepare it."

He noticed the journalists. "Hello, writers," he said to them. "Two of the commanders will be in to report later so you can get your 'human touch' and little anecdotes. It was a good day and tomorrow will be even better. Now if you'll excuse me, the press briefing is over and I'd like to indulge in classified tactics."

They took the hint and left. David relaxed into a red velvet armchair.

The intelligence officers briefed him on the city of Suez. As far as they could tell from the various reports, very little resistance could be expected. Troops were withdrawing from the area and the fate of the 3rd Army, cut off and surrounded, didn't encourage those who stayed behind.

Unexpectedly, after receiving word that the regiment commanders would be late, David declared, "Leave me alone with the spy. We'll have dinner, and I'll discuss tomorrow's plan with you later. You better get a couple of hours' sleep while you are excluded from our company."

The officers left smiling, and other than a redheaded soldier at the communication set, we were left alone. I found it amazing to realize how fond I had grown of a man I barely knew, in a matter of hours. He wanted to listen and I felt like talking.

"Son of a bitch Phoenix," he suggested for an opener. "I hope he is worth the trouble."

"Isn't everyone?"

"Not if he does it for money."

"How much do you want to know?"

"As long as we have the time, let's have the story. I have always been intrigued by you guys. Seems like a dumb game, but I know of occasional results, too. Also I appreciate a lonely game. I work with a group, we all do. We surround ourselves with sons and daddies. I have a cook who knows my taste, a driver who takes care of my intestines, batallion commanders who never question me and friends who can stand my dirty habits. Even this stinking velvet armchair pops up whenever we camp because I mentioned I was comfortable in it. I doubt how well I could operate alone. I have to feed and be fed. Even homosexuality I suspect to be better than masturbation."

I doubted he really wanted the whole story. I wasn't even sure how well I remembered the whole story.

I clearly recalled the original file. It had been handed to me, together with another four, at my Tel-Aviv desk. I was leaving for Europe and I had to choose one of the five. Someone who had the potential, who could be developed into a worthy operator. On my desk rested five lives, and I had the satanic power to take one of them in my hands, give it an identity and reshape it. Give it meaning but perhaps destroy it. It was a professional task then. Now I shuddered even thinking about it.

Is it age or a safety valve that makes my memory so

strangely selective? Marginal things—code names, passport numbers, aliases, names of cafes—I remember. Whole episodes, at the time constituting my entire life, are erased from my brain. Thus, with an effort, I tried to reconstruct the five files. What made me settle for Phoenix? The final choice was narrowed down to two. Phoenix and an American businessman. The American was a middle-aged retired millionaire, recently divorced and utterly bored with whatever affluence endowed him with. Ex-marine, a yacht owner, sports car collector and world traveler, he was looking for "something different." For excitement, a challenge, something youthful and active. He was the chief's candidate. He believed the man had the talent to survive and the freedom to detach himself. He asked me to examine the file carefully, discuss it with the psychologist and the graphology expert. He believed that the man was suitable for Saudia even if we started getting results only in a few years. Egypt was anti-American then, and he wouldn't have been welcome there in any capacity. The graphologist's report was rather positive. The man had courage, initiative and drive. What was lacking was depth and total sincerity. He left his wife, having tired of the attributes of marriage, in the hope that a blond secretary would arouse in him forgotten appetites. By the same token I feared he would leave us one day for other challenges. I remembered the report from our man in Madrid.

Rafi had met him in Ibiza, with the blond secretary, and recommended him. Rafi's recommendations resulted too often in disaster and this must have helped me make up my mind. The final touch was the chief's words, "Take good care of him, he's my baby. I almost drafted him in a Chicago sauna, both of us naked in a steam bath. If it works out, what a chapter his story could make in my autobiography." Phoenix was different. According to the book and the principles of the previous chief I would never have touched him. He was a classic example of a "redemption case." "Never take someone whose motivation is atonement. Criminals who seek forgiveness or deserters who want to be rehabilitated. We are not the Catholic church," he used to say, "and basically, we need brave people but within the normal human structure."

Phoenix's curriculum vitae was not complex. He was born in England during World War II. His mother was a nurse in a north London hospital. When the boy was fifteen his parents divorced, and he continued to live with his mother. He won a scholarship to the university, studied hydraulic engineering and held a job with a plant which manufactured pumps. In the university he was friendly with two Israeli students. In the summer of 1965 he visited the Middle East, part vacation, but doing market research for the firm. He liked Lebanon, where he had a schoolmate as well, and had stayed two weeks in a kibbutz in Israel.

There was also a report by a Shmuel from kibbutz Naot. He described the young man as eager to help, to share and to belong. He added that he was "very reserved and unemotional, diffident and self-conscious in a very British manner."

This visit took place six months before I examined the file, and it seemed that the youth, soon after his return to Britain, contacted the embassy and offered his services.

I couldn't remember his original name. I always thought of him as Phoenix and two aliases we made him use.

The graphology expert added, "Consistent, determined, unambitious, a loner with an undefinable sense of guilt."

I suppose I was attracted to the insignificance in his personality. He seemed ordinary enough, nothing fancy or lurid. School certificates and a report from the Israeli irrigation engineer who had gone to school with him and met him again in Israel showed genuine interest in his profession. He cared and knew. He was fascinated by achievements in the field in Israel, the water-carrier from Lake Tiberias down to the Negev desert, and visited some of the installations. What he lacked in experience was compensated by imagination and foresight.

There were other details. He had never been a party member and could be classified as a moderate conservative. His hobbies were chess and amateur radio. He had no passion for sport, food, drink or women.

So much has happened since that I can't place information or thoughts in a consecutive sequence. I do remember, however, that before I met him for the first time I gave much thought to his motivation. When he arrived in the embassy and offered his services, he was not the one who thought in clandestine terms. I rather liked that, having a deep objection to those who are set on playing cloak and dagger. The thrill he was after was merely professional, and his admiration for Israel, coupled with a personal ambi-

tion within his profession, was positive. He had no
hatred for the Arabs, or for that matter, knowledge of
them. No seeking of revenge. I never trusted those
who wanted to help us because they wanted to
damage the other side. Still, at that time, the real
driving motive was missing. Considerations crossed
my mind. Was he running away from something? Was
he, after all, after money, which he obviously lacked?
He wasn't an adventurer, but could he be the planted
innocent? One thing was clear. Water fascinated him,
the procuring of it, the pumping and the use of it, the
desalination processes and the power it produced. He
was a water-maniac and a thorough student of it. I
was always taken by technological dedication.

There were details I don't remember. Addresses,
phone numbers, a medical report, biographies of a
few friends.

A meeting was set in Paris; we are now in May,
1966. The purpose of the meeting was simple. I had to
find out whether he was willing, and fit, to do something he didn't intend—to work for us in Europe, go
through special training and eventually work under
cover in an Arab country.

I've had protégés before, so I was familiar with the
guidance and training involved. The last one I worked
with was a failure, against everybody's expectations.
He had all it took, and he never really betrayed us.
He wasn't even a spectacular disaster, just lost his
nerve at the crucial time. So I was rather reluctant to
start the routine, and being in a senior position it was
agreed that I'd control the new man, supervise his
"education" and watch out for his morale. The technical training could be done by a field worker. This

meant involving a third party, which we weren't
happy about. But it was understood that the two
would not work together or meet again once the
training was over.

Paris in May inspires everything but drafting a male
operator. The soft-scented air lay gracefully on the
city's shoulders, like a mohair shawl. The trees were
budding in the Tuileries gardens and the gilt statue
of Jeanne d'Arc gleamed in the afternoon sun as I
looked down the rue de Rivoli. At five sharp he appeared at the sidewalk cafe. Slightly shorter than I
imagined, he fit the physical description I had of him.
The cafe was half empty but he didn't bother to look
around. He knew he would be met and chose a seat,
stretched his legs and unfolded the *Herald Tribune*. I
crossed the street and pulled out a chair next to his.
I introduced myself, using a false name, and after the
inevitable preliminaries—the flight, the beauty of
Paris, and one café-filtre—I suggested we go for a
walk in the garden.

I decided to be as straight with him as I could. We
sat on a bench looking at the pond and I asked him—
something I never did—point blank: "Would you
consider, after suitable training, working for us in
Israel, or would you be prepared to help us in neigh-
boring countries, too?" He didn't seem surprised.
(Was he, after all, planted? He did have a Lebanese
engineer working with him.)

"In what capacity?" he asked. His eyes were deep
brown and he had an intriguing way of lowering them
when he asked a question and then staring me straight
in the eye when I answered.

"I don't know yet. That depends on circumstances. Economic and political."

"I wouldn't like to change my profession. Within the profession, I would like to contribute. I don't care what organization I work for or whether it's here or in the Middle East."

"Why the eagerness? You have a job, a country, a flat. What I'm talking about may involve a complete change in all these."

"I realize that. If we are sitting here and talking you must know all there is to know about me, so why should I add anything."

"You are not surprised at my offer?"

"It did cross my mind. Your man in London wanted to know more than any employer would ever dare ask." He didn't smile once. He wasn't nervous or ill at ease. He wasn't chummy, but he was fully present. A presence that is noticed only by the vacuum it leaves when it's gone.

"We are going to meet tonight. We'll have dinner and talk and you have time to think. Afterward we won't meet for a while, and then when we meet again we'll be working together."

We walked in opposite directions. He walked slowly, crossing the Concorde, and I took a side exit to rue de Castiglione. I felt tired and upset. He didn't ask questions, he wasn't curious, he didn't try to sell himself or advertise his talents. He was not excited or confused and it was all too matter of fact. I felt tired at the prospect of a long relationship with this man. There was ice to penetrate or melt and form again. Girls in pastel spring fashions attracted my eyes and I sipped a lemonade in a quiet bar. I didn't question my judgment as much as I questioned my own enthusiasm for the game.

He did smile when we met for dinner. He replaced his scarf with a necktie and looked fresh and attractive. He didn't like fish, so we went to a small bistro I knew in Montparnasse.

We talked mostly about water, his summer visit to Israel and his professional aspirations. These were the only subjects which interested him. Any deviation produced an expression of boredom on his face.

He was obviously admiring Israel for many wrong reasons. He respected our moral integrity and our virtuous dedication. He never scratched the surface, never questioned the self-advertised superlatives, yet he wasn't simpleminded or shallow. He wanted to believe. And that was as far as I could penetrate in my search for motivation.

It was the strongest, the simplest and thus the most difficult motive to accept. Only later, when I purposely tried to shatter it, did I discover it to be true, but later I knew facts I hadn't been aware of in Paris.

I stayed in a small hotel in the 16th arrondissement. The room was dark and quiet, the bed wide but uncomfortable. I spent a sleepless night trying to make up my mind. By dawn I reached a decision. He was to be trained and drilled, and whoever did it would add his opinion to mine. I didn't suspect disloyalty or lack of talent. I couldn't even place my doubt, though I suspected it had to do with lack of self-preservation. Not self-destruction. The man couldn't care less whether he lived or not. It was both a reason and a result of lack of human contacts, ties, commitments— the things that keep us all going. This, perhaps, made him perfect for the service, but it was an unknown, weird quality which frightened me.

For the six months that followed I was absent from his life, though he was not from mine. The technician who worked with him—a professional master—briefed me on his progress and completed the character report.

As far as Phoenix could gather, he was trained for some form of economic warfare. We were to combat the blockade the Arabs put on Israeli goods and foreign companies dealing with Israel, discover more about the blacklist, and eventually try to sell Israeli exports under different trade names to Arab countries. We tried to remain within his professional boundaries and learn more about his character. I was busy with other things and Phoenix was only on the fringes of my thoughts.

He was an Englishman attracted to our cause and willing to be of use, which he might or might not be. He was a natural with radio equipment, so we didn't waste time on communications training. If we had stopped there, he would have had no way of involving any of us. We didn't offer him a cover or a change of identity. What was there—open and straight—was good enough, and we took no risks.

Just before the second meeting we had a break. I was half intent on keeping his name on the list without using him much, when we came across the missing piece in the motivation puzzle.

The use of women, planted to obtain information, is rare and I don't encourage it. But by coincidence he knew an Israeli girl who was working for us so we decided to brief her and use her report. They had met in kibbutz Naot, and she had contacted him in London where she had gone to complete her studies. They met occasionally but he never told her about his meetings with me or with the other man. One Sunday she met his mother and returned with a strange report. The genteel, ordinary British nurse was more curious and knowledgeable about Israel than could be expected. She knew names of places, pronounced Hebrew words correctly and had a nostalgic sad attitude when Ofra, the girl, recounted stories about her own family.

During her next meeting with Phoenix she asked him whether his mother "was half Jewish or something" and out of the blue he said, "No, but I am."

Our sense of failure at not having obtained the information through our own methodical sources was cleared away by the information itself.

Phoenix's father was an Israeli, a soldier in Britain during the war. He met and loved the pretty nurse. At the same time that she discovered she was carrying his child, he was sent to North Africa and they lost touch. She married whomever she did and gave her son his name, and though she heard briefly from the real father later, she never told him about his son.

The father returned to Palestine, wrote a few letters about the country and its prospect of becoming a state, and was active in the underground against the British. When the nurse divorced, she tried to find her child's father only to discover he had been killed in the War of Independence. She decided not to disclose to Phoenix his real identity, but on his return from Israel, so enthusiastic and involved, she did.

Thus, when he reported to our London embassy he performed an act of homecoming, even if he—for reasons known only to himself—decided to keep it a secret. I didn't want him to know Ofra was my source, but I decided he should know I had this information. By then I had more than a vague idea of how we could really use his services.

When I met Phoenix in London I thought I had the upper hand. I knew something he didn't realize I knew. And I asked him about it, as if it were a sin or a crime he was trying to hide.

"I thought you knew," he said, and added it was his own business. He would have liked to work with us anyway, he said, whoever his father was. He wasn't sentimental about it, or apologetic about not bringing it up earlier. If this was the end of a string leading somewhere, to a search for identity, he was unemotional about it. I didn't pursue. I was comfortable in the thought that he was performing an act of homecoming, fulfilling an unwritten will of a father he never met.

"You must know about Ofra, too," he said.

"I know you are seeing her. That is none of my business—for the time being anyway."

We had two long talks. Mostly abstract, ideological. I told him about my own life, my commitments, my faith in what we were doing. Nothing factual, no planning of action, just the whys. He was a good listener, though he seldom asked questions. If he had doubts, he didn't share them. I believe he grew fond of me, for when we parted he made sure we were going to meet again. He was rather eager to start working.

CHAPTER 11

It was almost midnight before the battalion command-ers entered the war room. David greeted them with a hug and poured them coffee.

He hadn't interrupted my long story and I was wondering whether he was really listening or just relaxed with his own thoughts and plans while I was busy talking.

We were back to present time, and it was very easy to switch from foggy London to the outskirts of Suez.

The maps we had were not adequate. David point-ed to the roads leading to the city, marking with a red-and-blue marker the two axes he wanted his men to occupy by dawn.

He described the city as if he were a tourist guide. South of it was the sea, to the east a swamp area, and the west and northeast were only partly passable. There were several entrances to the city; the south would be attacked by another brigade from the Suez-Cairo road toward the port section—Port Ibrahim; south and west, near the refineries, would be taken care of by other forces, and we were to enter from the north. This approach was limited to the old road along the canal, which splits after its intersection with the sweet-water canal.

One battalion would continue along the beach, the other through the main street to the center of the city.

Intelligence information indicated a commando battalion in Port Ibrahim, defense forces—less than a brigade—in the city, and an unknown number of armed soldiers who had withdrawn into the city from surrounding camps and strongholds.

David pointed to some air photographs. The old center was all narrow alleys and cluttered houses; the south was more modern, with wider streets and taller buildings. There were several squares, a municipality building, a hospital and an administration building. The promenade along the beach had palm trees and a colorful domed casino.

"Our task," David said, "is to cut across the city and join our forces in Port Ibrahim." He was quite relaxed. Reports did not suggest strong resistance, and Egyptian prisoners confirmed the information.

He looked at me. "Are you with us?" I nodded.

"Daniel here is looking for someone. He may be in the modern suburb near the sweet-water canal you see in the air photo. He will have a few men with him and," he emphasized slowly, "he will not be in anybody's way. Make sure he enters the area when it's clean and ours. His code for the wireless is Bird. There will be an Arabic-speaking officer with him and they'll try to locate the address they have.

"You can report directly to me or to my second. Don't linger. It's a one-try affair, and if it doesn't work, you turn north and we meet here."

They talked and I listened. I remembered myself as a young, eager company commander in 1956. I had changed a great deal, no doubt, but the faith and conviction were still there. I looked at the map and could smell the dynamite and see the dust behind the tanks. I could feel my senses edge, the nervousness before a battle, the accumulation of facts unknown, absorbing and digesting them until they become part of memory. As if I'd been there already.

Was Phoenix really there? The blond from London whose life I manipulated for a short time, an engineer turned agent in Egypt, was he really in these new blocks of apartments, on the fifth floor behind sand sacks? Trying to operate a dead wireless set, waiting with a pistol in hand? Playing chess with himself, counting time? Sprawled dead on the floor—a foreigner not to be trusted in war? We were to assemble at 0430 and be on our way by 0500. The three men assigned to me had only a vague idea of what I was after. They were far from enthusiastic.

"Shouldn't you get some sleep?" I asked David.

"No, son. I'll sleep tomorrow night. I wish I knew more about the guts of this city."

"Sorry to have taken so much of your time before."

"Better tell me the end of it. What was Ofra like? And what did you want Phoenix to do anyway?"

"Ofra was pretty. Very delicate and fine. Long fingers, I remember, hazel eyes. A very quiet girl, she felt good in London. Naturally I had to stop their friendship long before I could use him. To my surprise she minded more than he did. She wrote him for a while, to his mother, then returned to Israel. I haven't seen her for years.

"Phoenix himself was phenomenal. He didn't have a life other than the life he had given us. He severed friendships, if he had any, and his mother didn't suspect his activities. He became a machine. His capacity to absorb information was enormous if unselective. He didn't question tasks, but improved on methods, and though never in real danger, he didn't ever try to avoid it, or seek comfort, or argue about money. The only thing he did without permission was to study Hebrew. In a month he was fluent in it, but swore he would never use it. He just had to understand and be able to speak it.

"I worked with him for a year. He took a few trips to Lebanon and Egypt, one to Jordan. He did stay within the professional bounds, but the scope was widened. It was a long-term investment, and we thought he could eventually take a permanent job in an Arab country. There was no filth. No meetings with freaks in secret apartments, no big money, no deep psychology or crisis. It was a productive healthy routine, almost dull."

Here David interrupted, "Do you really believe a guy like this could go all the way? Under pressure?"

"You can never predict that. He had a choice and took it, but I can't say he had the 'no-choice' mentality you and I have. He played the game."

"For us it is no game. When I make a decision I have behind it years of emotions piled up. I am not conscious of it, but there is King David watching me and Samson, the swamps my grandfather dried and the swamps my grandfather dried and the first orange trees my father planted. When I send men to battle, I remember the 1948 war and the 1956 campaign, the terrorists in the Negev and the Gaza strip and the Nazis in Europe. I remember the rich Jews in America and the assimilated ones in France. I have my own wife and grown-up children at my back, and the schools and the factories and the airstrips and the research institutes and the pretty girls on the beach and the folk songs and the spring flowers on Mt. Carmel. Whatever bloody theory you want to give it, all the things that compose love of country.

"He could never have all these. He had a father who died for it. A cerebral interpretation of Zionism and some knowledge of history. He was never subjected to anti-Semitism, he didn't have his favorite wadi in the Negev or alley in Jerusalem. He had never climbed Masada to see the sunrise over the Dead Sea, he hadn't necked with a girl, drunk with the smell of orange blossom in the spring."

"And yet you think he is waiting for us in an apartment ten miles from here with state secrets in his locked James Bond case."

"I don't know, David. Perhaps he escaped with the first sound of gun shots, but if he didn't and if he is there, we'd better get to him."

"What was he doing there, what was his assignment? He is no military expert, why wouldn't he clear out in case of war?"

"I left London, and Phoenix, and the whole secret scene for that matter, before 1967. By that time our man was a consultant to an Egyptian firm making purchases in Europe. He continued working for a British firm on a part-time basis. The man who took over from me, Gideon—you may have met him with Beni—worked with him for a few years and occasionally informed me of his whereabouts. The Egyptians developed powerful hoses. They figured they could penetrate the earth dikes with water if the stream were sufficiently strong. He succeeded in getting involved with the operation, pretending to believe their version claiming it was an agriculture project. Later they confided in him. His big cover was a claim for being money-minded. He was expensive and he spent it all on himself. In reports they refer to him as 'the dumb engineer.' It wasn't as much the technical information we were after, as the timing they had in mind. It was essential that he stay in the canal area when tension mounted, as he would be almost the first to know when they meant business.

"In 1970 we thought the whole thing was busted. He was sent to Israel by his British employer, to buy some irrigation equipment. He refused to decline the job, and there were many second thoughts. He claimed—and this I heard from Gideon later—that it added credibility to his dumbness and apolitical professional status. The truth was that he couldn't resist the offer and he arrived here. He didn't contact any of us, naturally. He stayed in a small hotel in Tel-Aviv, dined with the British commercial attaché, and made sure the whole trip was as short, business-like and successful as possible. There was one flaw. He made a trip to Beer-Sheba and met with Ofra. She was teaching, maybe still is, in the Ben-Gurion University and has a small apartment in the city. He spent a couple of hours with her, an evening, and returned to Tel-Aviv, to London and later to Cairo. It was decided to ignore this trip, as there was no indication of diminishing trust in him by the Egyptian company.

"It bothered me for a while. I didn't think he was playing a double game, but it was unlike him to leave a loose end, an emotional one, and Ofra obviously was not out of his system."

"So finally he didn't deliver, the bastard."

"If you mean this war, no. There were two false alarms but when the real thing happened, two and a half weeks ago, he was silent."

"Doesn't it make you wonder about the futility of the whole thing? You take a man, you train him for years, you risk the lives of strangers and contacts and families. You put money and effort and intellect into it, and you end with a stillborn baby."

"He was useful while he worked here. Small things, but not unimportant."

The finale must have upset David, for he claimed he had to work on the maps and suggested I get some sleep. I took the sleeping bag outside and lay on it on my back.

I hadn't told David everything. I didn't share my guilt with him. Phoenix was on my conscience more often than I'd like to admit. He hovered for a long while between me and Amalia. Every layer I shed, every step I made toward her, letting myself get involved, giving of myself, sharing with her, eventually falling in love—he was there. Not sarcastic or disapproving, but a whispering presence reminding me of what I had deprived him, shattering the monument I had built artfully to celibacy, independence and so-called freedom. Not on my wedding night, but in the moments of intimacy we built later,

when our love grew and we were self-sufficient, when
we didn't need words or actions to prove it, when I
blessed my good fortune—he was there. Almost naive,
not reproaching, just wondering what gave me the
right to tutor him into abstaining from all these joys.
I told myself I had nothing to do with his choice.
He was built that way; it wasn't my duty to turn
him into a sociable, caring human being. I had used
what had been there anyway. When my first child
was born, Phoenix reappeared in my mind. For the
first time in my adult years I had tears. I cried looking
at the baby. The helpless fragility, the vulnerable
little body seeking warmth and protection, the tremendous unbearable responsibility affected me in a way
I never believed possible. And the sudden enormous
wave of love for a creature, without a name or
definite shape as yet, threw me off completely.
Phoenix was there, never to experience what I did,
and his father was there too, ignorant of his son's
birth.

I almost talked to Amalia about him, but didn't.
I was afraid to admit I wished he would throw the
game away and stand in a maternity ward waiting
room, as I had done, not daring to touch his first
infant and holding back his tears. And this was precisely why I was going into Suez the next day. I hoped
he was alive, and well and cool and composed. I
would find him to prove us wrong. To tell him the
game was over and not worth it. To tell him to get a
job in Beer-Sheba and polish up his Hebrew, court
Ofra on desert nights and come home. Home could
never be codes and aliases and secret rendezvous and
messages, not even an occasional warm handshake

and the gratitude of the man in charge. We'll bring him home and he can desalinate the Red Sea and irrigate the desert or his own garden for all I cared. Or go back to England if that's what he wanted, or work for the Saudis if by now he has become truly money-minded. I wanted his shadow out of my life, and I did care for him enough to wish him some of the profound happiness that had befallen me.

The horizon was pale pink through the mist. The camp woke up, lazy for a brief second and jerking into full commotion in the next. There was a feeling of a last battle in the air, the final touch to a job already done.

Men took positions in their tanks, adjusting vests and helmets. The radio net was active and three men were saying their morning prayers next to a half-track. The sight was an unpleasant reminder of the day the war started. I clenched my fists. I wasn't even thinking about Phoenix just then.

David, who miraculously looked as if he had had a good night's sleep, walked with me to one of the jeeps.

"The driver speaks Arabic," he said. "Oren is a doctor. When your mission is over I may ask him to join the main force, if we need him. The machine gunner can handle the radio set. Just make sure you don't get lost, keep behind all the time, and report to me."

"Many thanks. I'll see you later."

"I'd like to meet your Phoenix one day, don't know why."

He turned to go, tranquil and confident.

"What a fighter," the driver said. The doctor was busy with his equipment, rearranging bandages and plastic infusion containers. We all had helmets on, and waited with the twenty-odd vehicles for the order to move so we could take our place at the end of the column.

"Look up!" the driver exclaimed. We all did, to watch the majestic dive of eight planes. They must have bombed targets in the city, for soon we saw them turning back, circling and diving again. When they disappeared the order was given and we were on our way, soon covered with the dust of the tanks and half-tracks in front of us.

All the physical elements were there. The sounds and the sights and the smells, yet something was missing. The men weren't alert. There wasn't the prebattle tension that follows high motivation. The eyes of the soldiers and commanders reflected fatigue rather than excitement, and the fatigue produced carelessness. Men stood up exposed in turrets and half-tracks. Many did not wear their helmets and a few were dozing off. The orders were quite clear—to advance only as long as the going was easy. It was no battle of Stalingrad. The war had been won and the 3rd Army surrounded. The city of Suez was important, but the attacking force was not to take too many risks. These orders were reflected in the faces of the fighters, as if it were one battle too many.

For a couple of hours we drove south, along deserted army camps and missile sites. Occasionally a few Egyptians could be seen hiding or waving a white flag. Most of these were unarmed and bursts of fire from our side were left unanswered.

We stopped a couple of miles outside of the city. The men were cheerful now. The enemy seemed to have simply evaporated. There was no resistance in the tremendously well-fortified area we had driven through, and soldiers spoke of "a victory parade in the main street of Suez." From a distance the city really seemed deserted and old-timers recalled accomplishing occupation of cities like Beer-Sheba and Lydda merely by driving in full force along the main street.

If I didn't participate in the premature celebration, it wasn't because of premonitions or doubts. My mission had little to do with the battle forecast. I looked at the map and it all seemed unreal. I had a vague description rather than an address, as if we were in the center of Tel-Aviv.

"Make a left turn after the intersection with the sweet-water canal, then another left and the third house on the right, second floor," etc.

We had some water and a quick breakfast, and shortly before ten o'clock received orders to advance.

We entered the built-up area. On our right were high-rise apartment buildings and an open space to the left. From among the buildings a few soldiers stared at us phlegmatically and hurried to hide. We reached the boulevard, a wide street with a railway between the lanes, and speeded up. On the half-tracks in front of us soldiers were snapping photographs and tank commanders were standing upright in turrets, while all tank decks were open with heads peeping out. There was no indication of any resistance; our jeep driver yawned and seemed utterly bored. The column moved along the two lanes on both sides of the rails, fast approaching the sweet-water canal.

"We'll stay on the left side," I said, "and take the first turn left after the intersection."

Just before the bridge we detoured a large bomb-crater, a result of this morning's air attack and though the vehicles in front of us slowed down, we bypassed them, crossed the bridge and split from the column, turning left into a track parallel to the canal. The radio operator repeated casually, "Bird turning left." The air raid had ruined the road we were on, and we had to hold fast to the seats as I urged the driver to hurry.

All forgotten faculties in my system were awake now. I was watchful and tense and concentrated. We took another left turn toward the water, and stopped in front of the third house. As we stopped, we heard a barrage of tank fire from the main road we had just left. The men jumped from the jeep for shelter, but the street we were on was dormant and empty.

The two soldiers remained near the jeep, and I asked the doctor to follow me. We advanced along the white wall, holding on to the machine guns and bending over, through a deserted garden to the entrance hall. The house was not hit directly, but the doors were off the hinges and heaps of furniture were piled up near the windows. The ground floor was empty, and we climbed the cement stairs to the top floor.

There, too, the door was open and we stopped at the threshold. I was breathing heavily, and my excitement gave way to reality. The apartment was empty. The windows were shattered, the cupboards wide open. The iron bed had no mattress on it, and the kitchen and lavatory looked unused. There were

English newspapers on the balcony, but no definite evidence as to when Phoenix had left or whether he ever had been there.

From the balcony we could see clouds of black smoke from the intersection, and hear the consistent, growing sounds of small arms fire and artillery shelling. I was thinking fast now. There seemed to be no point in proceeding to the water plant, a mile away, as the apartment seemed to have been deserted for a long while, perhaps used recently by soldiers. The driver called us from below, slightly panicky as the sounds of a fierce battle reached him. We had to move on.

I asked the radio man to report to David, "The bird was not in the nest." The reply was a curse with an order to return.

CHAPTER 12

Very seldom in life had I had to make a major decision
in a matter of seconds. My mission was over. Phoenix
was not there, alive or dead, and I had to return north.
I could turn right and arrive at Faid airport in an
hour. Fly to Tel-Aviv, report and be at home for
dinner with Amalia and the children. There was a
cease-fire and the war was over and my little contribution was over, too. We could see the main street
now. In its midst two of our tanks were on fire and
other vehicles were looking for shelter. Men from
troop carriers were running toward the alleys, shooting and being shot at. Other vehicles were driving in
the opposite direction stopping to load the wounded.
The doctor exclaimed, "Good God, no!" And as we
reached the main street I instinctively pushed the
driver's hand to the left, to the center of town where
all hell seemed to break loose.

There was little time to assess the situation. The
column was under intense fire from all directions,
R.P.G.'s were fired from the alleys, bazookas were
active on the rooftops and windows and whoever was
exposed, as most of the commanders were, were hit.
The fire was direct, combined with efficient hand

grenade hits and for a second it seemed like a hopeless trap from which no man was to emerge alive. In ten minutes most of the vehicles were hit, and the voices on the radio were hysterical. I could hear crews reporting the deaths of their tank commanders, and for a few seconds no orders were given, just casualty reports. The city, which had seemed empty and defeated when we drove in parade-style, turned into an inferno.

The jeep was useless. I told the men to jump off and we crawled into a half-track which had been hit but was still operational. On its floor wounded soldiers moaned, and I helped the doctor transfer them to the jeep. Our driver was going to evacuate them using the route we came in on, which seemed safe enough.

The driver of the half-track was in shock but unhurt, and I told him to get moving. There was enough ammunition in the vehicle, three men who were not hurt and the three of us, including the doctor.

The tank behind us was hit and caught fire and its crew signaled us to stop. We managed to collect them and start moving just as the tank exploded. The doctor was busy now, and I had to decide on a course of action. There was the danger of a hand grenade hitting us directly. We had no top-cover and I warned the men to look out for grenades. Our own fire was efficient now. The men shot at definite targets. Men in windows, in alleys, on the roofs. As long as we were in motion we could almost control our path. The men resumed a fighting mechanism drilled into them for years. They switched back from the apathy that followed the surprise into the aggression of self-defense, and though we didn't know each other's names, within a few minutes we worked as a trained homogeneous unit. My own feelings alternated momentarily. There was something absurd in the situation, and I felt like an idiot and a hero according to the progress we made.

The boulevard was two miles long. On both sides now were five-story buildings, and the general idea was to reach the large square at its end where we could meet the rest of the force. Each vehicle had a "private battle," each unit using its common sense and judgment on how to advance and avoid being surrounded. There were tens of Egyptians in each of the cross-alleys, so the only chance was to stick to the main street. Men whose vehicles were hit ran for shelter into buildings and behind fences. It was difficult to read the battle as a whole. More and more I realized we were not attacking a city, but trying to save our own skins. My main concern was not to be cut off from whatever was left of the slowly-moving column.

The hysteria on the wireless calmed now, and clearer orders were given—avoid alleys, raise flags when evacuation of casualties was essential. Toward noon we received some air support. Tank commanders were nominated to replace the dead, and sergeants and corporals took over from majors and captains. The intensity of the battle did not let up, and there was no time to think.

From where I sat I looked at my men. The doctor had bandaged his own shoulder, one man was dead and clumsily covered on the floor, and one of the adopted tank-crew fighters suffered from severe burns. We were out of water, and I ordered the men to be careful with ammunition as we had run out of hand grenades.

We weren't getting anywhere. It was impossible to keep up with the tanks, and the infantry on half-tracks dispersed or barely moved. We had firepower but no mobility, and whoever came to a complete stop was soon surrounded by Egyptian soldiers and had to fight a face-to-face battle.

I had to replace the driver whose hand was hit and bleeding. He crawled back to the doctor who was running out of bandages, and the tank driver took his seat. Two minutes later the front part of the half-track was hit by a grenade, the engine stopped, and I ordered the men to jump out and run into a house on the street corner which seemed unoccupied. I covered their retreat. Dr. Oren supported the badly burnt case, and together with the driver we joined them, carrying the corpse covered with a blanket. When we reached the entrance hall we heard our vehicle explode, and I sent two of the men to explore the building. Short bursts of machine-gun fire indicated resistance, but my men shouted that the second floor was clear now and we could join them. We pulled the wounded to one of the rooms and the men who were unhurt protected the front and top of the building. Our entrance there must have been ignored, for no fire was directed at us and we could get organized. The account I gave myself of our position was not very pleasant. We had no communication set and no water. Oren was short on everything and ran out of antibiotics. We all had machine guns but very little ammunition, and though the Egyptians didn't know we were there, neither did our own forces. There were still three hours of daylight and there was no way of moving before dark. Water and morphine were top priority, and realizing the risk, I sent two men through the back entrance to try and acquire them. Any of our deserted vehicles might have a supply, and they might be able to contact another trapped unit with a radio set. It was a hot day and the smoke and fire increased the thirst. The men came back with a gerry-can of water and some bandages. Two houses away there were some paratroopers and they expected us to join them with nightfall. Together we should be able to get out of here during the night.

Stench hung in the air of the room where the wounded were. I forced myself to stay for a while.

On the back of the map I jotted down their names and addresses. Only one of them was a reservist, the others were youngsters, though veterans of many battles during the last three weeks. The burnt man was attached to an infusion bag and bandages covered his face and both hands. I thought of Amalia, very briefly, as if a slide of her in a white apron was projected too quickly on the dirty wall, two-dimensional. Two of the men were hurt in the legs and couldn't walk, one suffered from a severe loss of blood and was in terrible pain. The last dose of morphine was administered to him. A young blond boy was scratched superficially, but he was in a state of shock and Oren motioned to me to leave him alone. I talked to them briefly. This was no place for long lectures and banalities. We were all tired and only honesty was acceptable. I explained to them where we were and how we were planning to get out of there, "So rest and pray and be patient."

We moved the corpse to another empty room, and I added his name and identity number to my list.

His name was Arik. Only then I remembered Phoenix's original name, which oddly had escaped me all along. His name in the file was Eric Berkov. I remember saying to him once, "When you live in Israel, when the job is done, they'll probably call you Arik."

I walked up to the top floor. The two men I sent there had orders not to shoot unless we were spotted. They were crouching behind the parapet where I joined them.

"Where is your battalion?" the redhead asked me.

"I have no battalion."

"So what are you doing here? Looking for someone?"

"Precisely. Only I didn't find him."

"Your son or something?"

"No. A man who worked with me. A foreigner."

"He was smarter than us."

I was grateful they didn't pursue the matter. Phoenix was irrelevant now. I brought them some crackers and jam and we shared a cigarette. There were two corpses in the corner of the roof—the enemy they had surprised when they climbed up and shot from the back.

"How are the wounded doing?" asked the redhead.

"Alive. We are fortunate to have a doctor with us. With nightfall we'll join the paratroopers in the next alley and try and clear the hell out of here."

"That's another two hours. We could use some sleep."

"You can sleep in turns."

The second soldier was a Yemenite, dark-skinned and sad-eyed. He looked very young, younger than the others. He was silent all along and suddenly asked me, "Are you married?"

"Yes. Two young sons. Why?"

"I am getting married next week. If we get out of here."

"Of course we'll get out of here. Where do you live?"

"In Rehovot, but we are going to get a farm when I am out of the army. I studied in an agriculture school."

"How old are you?"

"Nineteen, and don't tell me, what's the hurry . . . look at us here, with perhaps five minutes, or one hour to live. So, I am in a hurry."

A head appeared in the roof entrance signaling me to come down.

"I'll be back when it's time to move. Take care and lie low." There was something comforting in these two. Not overconfident, just wanting to survive and remaining cool and composed about it. With only so few years of life behind them it seemed remarkable. The redhead smiled and winked and lit his last cigarette.

On the ground floor the morale was improved. The men ate and drank and adjusted to their new predicament. Rescue was feasible, and the despair of the trapped with which they were infected at first seemed to have disappeared. Soldiers who had been thrown together by accident began to feel the intimacy of shared fate, which produced confidence and broke their solitude.

Three of the soldiers were talking in whispers in a

corner. They smiled at me and I smiled back. They were children. What did they think of me? Did I inspire them with confidence? Did they think I was an inexperienced office-colonel? I didn't really know them. They belonged to another generation, they used a different jargon. Did they care about the same things we did?

I sat next to them, though I wanted to be alone.

"Won't be long now," I said with confidence. "You'll help with the wounded, we have to improvise a couple of stretchers from the doors and blankets here."

"Don't worry," one said. "We'll all get out of here."

They offered me half a bar of chocolate. This reminded me of a supply I had in my bag. I took out a flask of whiskey and some sweets intended for Phoenix. He didn't drink, but I thought it might please him in these weird circumstances.

They looked at each other. Whiskey was a luxury and I had to explain myself.

"I was sent here to look for a friend. An Englishman. I brought him this but he wasn't there so we might as well enjoy it."

We had a drink. None of us seemed to like the taste but believed it would do us good.

"A cocktail party," one said. "Only the ladies are missing."

"The ladies are waiting at home."

None were married. I found myself talking about Amalia and my boys.

"You really met with the Six Day War? This time there were no girls in the front line."

They talked about the wounded in the other room. They considered themselves lucky.

"Burns are the worst. Face, hands, the parts that are exposed."

"Would you rather lose a leg or a hand?" one asked.

A macabre conversation followed. Is blindness better than the loss of legs, is there a wound that is worse than death?

"Cheerful, aren't you," I muttered.

"Don't take us seriously. We've been through all this before. It just makes time pass and then we are grateful for staying alive and in one piece."

"Try to get some sleep. In an hour we'll start preparing for departure."

I crawled to the front door. I was lying on my belly trying to get a look at the street. Two of my soldiers were behind the fence. They couldn't see me, but they seemed relaxed and comfortable. The remains of two vehicles were still burning in the middle of the street, but the buildings across looked deserted. From the distance there were sounds of sporadic fire and occasional artillery. There was no imminent danger to my small group, but there was no way of telling what hid behind the next corner.

I was tired. I felt I could lie there, legs stretched and hand resting on the machine gun, for many hours.

On the roof, in front, inside, were men who accidentally became my responsibility. I felt out of place but not unfit to cope. I missed my own unit and friends. The jokes we shared, the nicknames, the security we gave each other. In 1956 I lay like this for twenty-four hours. Next to Beni. We didn't talk much, never discussed possible wounds or death, but I was sure he would never leave me behind. Our hearts beat in the same rhythm and we shared convictions, loves and resentments. I didn't think we were better fighters or driven by nobler causes, but the familiarity I was used to was missing. I moved carefully inside. The sun was setting, and I went to see the doctor.

"We'll need two stretchers. The rest can walk with help."

"I hope the paratroopers in the next building can give us a hand in evacuating. Unless they have casualties of their own."

"We'll also need a stretcher for the dead man."

The soldier with the chest wound was trying to tell me something. I bent down and put my ear next to his mouth.

"Someone will have to account for all this."

"Account for what?"

"For this bloody battle. Two of my pals were killed, and so was my commander who was the nicest guy in the army."

"So this is war."

"And the war was over, and we had enough of it and when I recover I will want to know that this battle was essential, that it made one bit of difference."

Oren told him he shouldn't be talking.

"There will be enough time for that, when we are out and well. Don't strain yourself now."

The man shut his eyes but his lips continued moving.

"I wish I had the medications I need."

"We have an hour to go. Do you feel the way he does?"

"Who can tell? Perhaps every other battle is superfluous. We can never find out in advance how the whole thing would end without it, how each battle affects the future borders and the political setup. They are young and have had more than a fair share of fighting. They carry with them sights of best friends killed and the fear of their own death or disability. Too many commanders were killed. They were trained to follow excellent leadership."

"The same in other wars."

"Didn't you ever doubt the absolute necessity of a battle, or the validity of an order?" Oren asked me.

"Not really. It never lasted that long though and I was always surrounded by men who had experience and deep integrity. I'll take care of the stretchers, and send a scout to the next house in twenty minutes or so."

Did I have that flawless conviction I wanted to take for granted in others? We didn't want automatic obedience. We encouraged initiative and imagination, but could we afford the doubts? Did we spread the shoulders wide enough for the burden?

The burden of memory. Somehow I expected every youth to charge with the support of Moses and Abraham, Isaac and Jacob. I expected them to be inspired by King David's courage and King Solomon's wisdom, and to be motivated by years of Diaspora persecution. On these dirty Suez house walls I wanted them to read the warnings. Warnings in blood and smoke and blue and white. The pogroms in the Ukraine which sent my great-grandparents, theirs, too, perhaps, with bundles in deep snow on roads from nowhere to another nowhere. I could see the boats, not seaworthy, flung by waves making their way to Palestine, decks crowded with praying immigrants, and they were stubborn and noble and miserable. On the floor reflected in broken glass I could see the footsteps of Jews lined up to the gas chambers and slaughterhouses, and every barbed wire I cut or crawled under in past battles was a reminder of ghettos and concentration camps. The load of memory had a sound to it, of prayers and songs, soft weeping of orphans and crude laughter of anti-Semites, songs I cherished as a teen-ager around a bonfire composed during the War of Independence, songs we sang in the Sinai in the other wars—conceited and victorious. The echoes of Kaddish said by sons over fathers' graves, by fathers at sons' funerals. Songs of sorrow, of hope, songs of promise and dreams.

The burden of memory that pushes the tank chains and adds fuel and speed to the flight of the fastest jets, the sights and sound and smells of thousands of years which somehow were with me in every fight, skirmish or battle. Did they all feel it? Did the redhead think or know of the ghetto in Warsaw? Did the Yemenite carry traces of anti-Semitism in San'a? Did it matter? What if I had only a picture of Amalia, Rani and Ofer? What if I thought only of my Tel-Aviv neighborhood and the white table in the kitchen set with a bowl of spring flowers or summer fruit? Would I have run away then, or been less motivated? Out of nowhere, from the corner, as if he were reading the doubting look in my eyes as I measured him, one of the boys said, "I was thinking of Anne Frank. How they were stuck in an attic for weeks, with the Nazis outside. That really took courage."

I climbed the stairs to the roof. The Yemenite greeted me with the widest of smiles. The redhead looked at his watch. "Time to go? I kind of like it here. Most rest I've gotten in a month."

"You'll stay until we are ready and packed. When we leave the building you cover the street for five minutes and follow immediately. We'll wait for you with the paratroopers. In the room below we'll lay the corpse of your dead friend on a stretcher and tie it up. You'll take it. If you are under fire, leave it and seek cover, and that's an order. We can get it later."

"His mother would love this."

"Your mother wouldn't like it any other way."

I explained to them the route we were going to take, through the back door, across an alley and into the backyard of the next corner building.

Below, the men were getting ready. Checking arms and ammunition, lacing shoes and putting on shirts. Oren checked the stretchers, they were heavy but safe.

"If we are lucky we'll get a couple of light ones from one of the stuck half-tracks."

Two of the wounded practiced walking, clenching fists in pain. I signaled to the two men in front. They came in, drank some water, and listened to my last orders. One of them would leave first. "He will go to the other house and back, make sure the path is clear. Then we'll leave with the casualties. The stretchers with the doctor, and myself with those who can walk with support. The boys from the roof will follow."

It was growing darker, and we had to get our bearings before complete nightfall. We were now at the back entrance, facing an inner yard.

"Hold your fire, whatever happens, and good luck," I said. The scout left us, quick and wiry, and disappeared behind the outer wall. I looked at my watch and timed him. The next ten minutes lingered like an hour. The wounded were uncomfortable and the others nervous, each one wrapped in thoughts or hopes, separate worlds thrown together into a backyard of a Suez apartment building. I felt paternal. I wasn't worried, the odds were for us, and I'd been through tougher moments. So had they, but the futility of the whole operation and the last few hours left them at the edge of their patience. I looked at the burnt man. The bandages covered his face but his dry lips were moving. It crossed my mind that I could now grasp Amalia's resentment of being touched. I looked at my watch, five minutes passed. He should be on his way back already. Did they think of women? I knew preoccupation of men with sex in battle to be a fallacy. We thought of women as the clean, almost ethereal entity representing everything that was not battlelike. We thought of their voice, eyes, soft hair, of dresses with frills, or dressing gowns or bathing suits and small feet in sandals. We were too tired to want to jump into bed, we wanted to be caressed and fondled and put to sleep.

In the silence we could hear fast footsteps. Automatically I directed my gun, but our own soldier appeared, breathing heavily.

"It's clear. But we have to hurry. The others are ready to leave. There is an Egyptian post to cross and half a mile to walk. The medics and two vehicles are waiting for us at the intersection. The paratroopers have their own wounded and two dead and can't give us a hand but their radio is working and they have some morphine and an empty stretcher."

The doctor adjusted the infusion bags, the last he had, and the first group was on its way following the boy who had just returned.

I made the soldier with the leg wound lean on me.

"I can try and hop on one leg," he whispered.

"Save your energy for later. You may need it." He had a stick to lean on and we started on our way. His name was Haim. He was thin and we managed well, but he was concerned.

"I'm slowing you down."

"Shut up. You are lighter than a bazooka or a stretcher."

Oren said, "They may save the leg if we get there on time." I hushed him. I could hear behind me the footsteps of the men from the roof.

The paratroopers were waiting. Their commander was on a stretcher. He had lost a lot of blood but refused morphine and kept the morale of his men high and almost humorous all along.

We decided to move in groups of two or three. Three men would lead and cover from the front. The wounded were to follow, and I would cover with three men from the back. There were enemy soldiers on the second floor of the next building. We could hear them talking but they behaved as if the show were over. There was an alley to cross and a long street to follow. We figured it might take us up to two hours to reach our forces.

The first three left, swift like alley cats, and the others began to move. Haim stayed with me and awaited our turn.

In front of us two injured soldiers were supporting each other. They had minor injuries but were weak and slow. I waited for them to disappear behind the corner and Haim leaned on his cane ready to go. He was very pale, as far as I could judge in the dark, and his pain increased as he hopped along. The blood stained the bandages and the temporary cast.

"I feel faint," he said. "I think you'd better leave me here."

I felt the weight of his body growing heavier, and stopped. Two hundred yards to cross into relative safety. We were now within range of the Egyptian post. I could see their cigarettes being lit and hear them. The men in front made it to the long alley which seemed empty. The redhead and his friend carrying the corpse caught up with us.

There were four of us. And a dead man. Haim was holding back sighs of pain.

I untied the dead man and laid Haim on the stretcher. The two others lifted him and I motioned them to go on as quickly as they could. "Don't wait for me. Get him to the doctors fast. I'll make it, and don't worry, I'll bring him along."

"Him" was wrapped in a blanket. I lifted the body on my back but it slid back and fell with a thump on some broken glass. The noise attracted the Egyptians and one of them looked through the window. I lay down next to the corpse and held my breath.

The Egyptian said something to his friends, they laughed and very casually he pressed the trigger sending what seemed to be the longest burst of machine-gun fire in our direction.

I could have shot him dead. He didn't see me but his silhouette was clearly framed in the window. He was within my range and my finger was on the trigger. It was obvious that he wasn't aiming. He didn't see us and probably thought the noise was made by a stray dog or cat. Shooting would have been stupid and I controlled myself. He joined his friends, laughing, and I felt the warm wetness of blood spreading between my chest and my shirt.

I had to get out of there before I could find out where I was hit, and if I was losing blood—before I lost too much. Still lying on my belly, I loaded the corpse on my back so his head was resting on my shoulder. I half-rose and on tiptoes, now feeling a throbbing pain somewhere along the shoulder blade, ran along two buildings, crossed the alley and half-collapsed in the narrow street which stretched far and empty, north into the intersection where someone perhaps waited for me.

I sat there for a few minutes. My left hand was in pain and useless and I unbuttoned my shirt, feeling for the wound. The bullet hole was in my left shoulder. Above the heart, above the lung, but bleeding and painful. I had no bandage and didn't manage to take my shirt off. I dug into the pockets of the dead soldier. I found a roll of flannel, used for cleaning guns. I pressed it hard against the wound which increased the pain, occupied my free hand and didn't entirely stop the bleeding.

"Silly idiot," I said to myself, and almost managed a smile. "What a way to die."

I wasn't dying and didn't think of death as more than a remote possibility. I checked the hand grenade that was tucked in my belt, an instinctive if slightly melodramatic reaction to the thought of being taken prisoner.

My head felt heavy then very light when I heard footsteps. The redhead was coming toward me, followed by the doctor.

"It's nothing, just a scratch," I managed to whisper.

"Don't worry. They are only five minutes away. We heard the shots."

They had a stretcher with them and Oren examined me quickly, adjusting the flannel roll I was holding and tying it with a wide bandage.

"The bullet you'll take with you to the hospital," he said.

They put the dead soldier on the stretcher and helped me on top of him. The load didn't seem to bother them. As if we were two feather blankets they lifted us up, silently and efficiently, and carried us along the alley into a half-track which started moving instantly. I must have had my eyes shut for when I opened them Oren was injecting my arm and David's irregular features were somehow floating not far from my face.

"So you lost a Phoenix and got yourself a bloody hole in the chest. I thought we had an understanding, something about turning back. I waited for you, son."

Whatever had been injected into me had resulted in less pain, drowsiness and a certain lightheartedness. I was almost happy.

"Where are we?"

"On our way to Faid airport. They'll bandage you properly and send you to a decent hospital."

"His real name was Eric. Eric Berkov."

"Screw him. The kids here say you are quite a guy, Cool, they say. Next time you join me on the first day."

"They weren't so bad themselves and there won't be a next time."

"So you say. I talked to your wife. I promised her we'd get you to the central hospital. She is waiting for you. Beni will see you in Faid."

"Come now. Don't give me a hero's funeral. Is the cease-fire effective?"

"Yes, and the bargaining may begin. We don't have the city, but the 3rd Army is isolated and thirsty and we have dug into this chunk of Africa where it hurts."

"How many casualties yesterday?"

"Too many. Rest calm now or Oren will transfer me to another car."

I shut my eyes and felt David's hand on my right hand. An unaccountable wave of human warmth engulfed me with his touch.

I vaguely remember being lifted again, bandaged and cleaned. There was a mixture of anxiety and matter-of-fact medical statements in the voices in the background. I could hear the chopper's engine start and I woke up with takeoff and another injection.

"You schmuck," Beni said. "I have to take you home on a stretcher, just great."

"It's nothing. How is Haim?"

I couldn't hear his answer for the noise, but I gathered he didn't know who I was talking about.

"Amalia called. I stalled her the first night, said you were listing tanks in the field. She said something about a Berkov. Someone you know."

I heard the name and tried to lift my head. "What about Berkov? I can't hear you."

He raised his voice and came closer.

"It doesn't matter now. He is dead. Died in the

hospital. She said he was there a while, unidentified or something. Later, I thought this was the fellow you were looking for. Gideon confirmed it, but it was too late to get to you."

"It makes no difference. I had to stay there anyway. What time is it?"

"Not midnight yet. I'll get off in Refidim, you are in good hands now and I'll come and visit you. Kiss Amalia for me, she is quite a girl."

We landed and he got off into the dimly lit camp. A few people climbed into the helicopter. The engines were running all the time and I fell asleep as we took off again.

I woke up as we were landing. Amalia's face filled the frame of my mind. Her small features and bright eyes, soft hair and knowing, slightly worried smile.

I'm home, I felt, from the longest short voyage, please hold me.

The wind blew in as the door was lowered. There were people and hands and white aprons and in their midst was Amalia, my wife, my love.

BOOK THREE

Amalia

CHAPTER 13

I was restless and couldn't sleep. For a good reason. The radio news reported renewed fighting in Africa, without being specific. I failed to get Beni's Headquarters on the phone, and when I did reach him, long past midnight, I was really worried.

Daniel wasn't with him.

"He is in the field, spending the night with a tank battalion."

"But I hear the battle is still on."

"Just clearing up resistance pockets."

"Beni, tell me the truth."

He was embarrassed for me. I talked as if my husband were the only man in the front line. What's more, I was indirectly accusing him.

"Listen now. The name of the game is war. Daniel knows the rules and isn't a newcomer, even if he did join only today. As far as I know, you don't have to worry more than the next wife or mother, so get a good night's sleep and take care of the children, and bake a cake when he returns." I tried to calm down. He was right, of course, and I felt selfish and spoiled.

"Tell him Arik Berkov is dead. I think he knew him. Tell him he was our unidentified patient."

"When I see him."

"Tell him I love him. Take care, you too."

His good-night was warm and reassuring. I opened the shutters and the pale light of dawn streamed in reluctantly.

I began to grasp the courage of what Julie referred to as the waiting women. What if he had left at the beginning? How could they stand the uncertainty, their ignorance of what was happening, the wild fears of the worst? I didn't want to think. I walked into the kitchen and prepared coffee and breakfast, and with a cup in my hand sat on Ofer's bed.

There was a battle on, and Daniel was there. There were bullets that pierced lungs, and shells that left men amputated or dead. There were missiles that burned tanks and sent Avi and Arik and others to Ward L, and now it wasn't happening to somebody else with me as a sympathetic observer. It was happening to me and my children, on this last day of the war, after the cease-fire had been declared.

It was chilly in the room. I adjusted the blankets and touched the heads of my boys.

Right now, this minute, he could be hit. How could other wives take it? Did they sit like this, minute by minute for eighteen days and nights, waiting for the phone to ring or for someone to arrive, smiling at the children and keeping themselves busy in the kitchen?

I wished I could pray. Explain to someone up there that we are just at the beginning of something, still searching. That it can't be severed here because we have a long way to go together.

Rani mumbled something in his sleep. I held his soft limp hand and he responded with a smile.

Suppose the phone rings, I thought and shivered. Would I have the strength to answer it?

They don't announce death by phone, I said to myself. They come to the door, with a doctor and tranquilizers and an officer in uniform brings the news. They ask you to sit down so if you don't know what brought them to your door . . .

A widow and two orphans. "War widow." As if it made a difference. As if terminal cancer or a fatal road accident were less welcome than a sophisticated Egyptian missile. I knew women who had lost their husbands in the War of Independence. "Their death gave us life," they were told. They remarried, but went to the cemetery on Memorial Day. A second cousin of mine lost her husband in the Six Day War. She didn't come to my wedding because she was mourning her dead and her baby son grew up without a father. In her home there were photographs of her husband everywhere, books and objects he liked became exhibits. The house was like a small shrine to his memory, and so was her life. I paid her a cordial visit once, then again, and no more. Recently someone told me she was thinking of remarrying. In a country of war, young widows are not a scarce sight, which doesn't diminish the personal tragedy. There were stories in each family, about widows who sank into self-pity, while others were criticized for forgetting too soon. There was talk of friends who had filled the house and then, one by one, stopped coming, of children who adjusted and others who became neurotic and difficult.

I reproached myself for even thinking that way. I was playing a drama with an idea, knowing so well that, in fact, if it did happen, it would be something entirely unknown to me. I still had the luxury of resenting exaggerated presence. What did I truly know about absence? The absence of a friend, a lover, the clothes in the cupboard and the shaving kit in the bathroom, the shoulder in bed, the hand on the beach, the quarrels and the joys and the knowing looks, the soft and the hard words, the little resentments and the compromises. The absence of the father of small children. Daniel's absence from the growing up of Ofer and Rani. This was an unbearable thought, and my cheeks were suddenly wet with tears. There was no one at the door, I said, almost aloud, and I was a selfish, self-indulging fool. It was time to wake up the boys and to begin the busy hour until they were off to kindergarten.

Ofer asked whether Daniel would return today, Rani repeated whatever his brother said.

"In a few days probably."

"Will he kill anybody?"

"I doubt it. He'll tell you all about it when he returns."

I took them down and drove to the hospital, slightly ashamed of my morning hysteria.

The hospital commander asked to see me. The major from Absentees was with him.

"Are you sure about the name?"

He was talking about No. 7. There was to be a funeral, and he wanted more than a hunch to go by.

"I think my husband knew him. If he did, you can

check with the service and get some more details. What we have seems to check."

He talked about the irregularity of the inquiry. In what capacity was I involved, he wondered, and why wasn't he informed of the diary earlier? It would be terrible to bury someone and then have him show up alive and well, and be left with an unidentifiable corpse.

I suggested he get in touch with Gideon, who had taken over from Daniel. He might know something. I was tired and not very helpful and he dismissed me. The funeral would leave at ten, anyway.

I walked into the ward. No, there hadn't been a phone call for me. Avi said I looked sick and offered me his bed as he was about to try the wheelchair.

"The battle of Suez is on," he said. "If this isn't the last one, don't hire me as a strategist."

"I am worried about Daniel."

"Let the man free for a couple of days. You were uncomfortable with him here, now you are anxious to see him back. Women!" he added.

I walked to the hospital's funeral house. The many people gathered there didn't show up for Berkov's last voyage. The Rabbi pointed to a command car with a wooden coffin on it. On both sides soldiers were sitting and two of the doctors from the ward waited in a car, ready to follow. I joined them.

It was rather irregular. For all we knew, the man in the coffin could be someone else. The autopsy didn't disclose much, and the service only confirmed there was an Eric Berkov working for them. They wouldn't give details, they would go into it next week or later.

The man in charge was himself wounded and in the hospital.

It occurred to me that nobody bothered to find out whether he was Jewish. The name was Jewish, all right, or could be, but these were not ordinary days.

"Does it matter?" the young doctor said. "He was killed in our war. He had no business fighting in the Sinai if he wasn't Jewish. There are no relatives or friends, and if one day this turns out to be an error, he can be transferred. We are not burning him or dissecting him, just letting him rest in peace with honors reserved to dead soldiers."

The command car moved and we followed, slowly and patiently. Not since Amnon's burial had I been to the cemetery. I bought flowers at the gate and we parked the car. I felt numb, as if it was all a bad dream or a surrealistic movie. The ceremony was short, and I could hear the words echo back from other graves and other groups of mourners. I laid the flowers next to the provisory sign saying "Arik Berkov" and we walked back to the car to listen to radio news. I don't know what made me say it but I did. "My husband is in Suez."

"What brigade is he with?"

"I don't know. It's a feeling I had, that's all."

"Try a healthier one."

"Do you know any girls' names beginning with 'O'?"

"Why? Are you expecting a baby daughter?"

"This Arik Berkov. There is a girl in his diary. She lives in Beer-Sheba, he calls her 'O'. He was somewhere abroad and returned here to be with her."

"Put an ad in the paper. Could be Orna or Olga or Ophina or Ofra or Osnat."

"I once knew a girl called Ohela," the other doctor volunteered.

"I'll wait for my husband, he may know more."

"What else was there in the diary?"

"Not much. Apologetic mostly. Full of clues to someone who knows and almost meaningless otherwise."

Back in the ward I did some errands for the head nurse, and drove home in time to prepare lunch for the boys. My neighbor's husband was home on a twenty-four-hour leave. She asked me in to share a cake. She looked pretty and young and I felt happy for her. And jealous. I was beginning to understand something profound. Something I had ignored or taken for granted, about myself and Daniel, the family and the depth of feelings and dependence.

My mother came over, but I was impatient with her. She took the boys out for a walk and I sat at the desk with Berkov's diary again.

He had to see "O," he wrote. If he had a strong feeling for her, and if it were mutual, nothing else mattered. What's more, there was nothing much in what he called "the water business," and no signs of a crisis that should prevent him from taking a few days off. A theory followed, about the space his work took in his life, or could, should it ever change. Were there "right" proportions, percentages that should be devoted to a job, a family, a country, friends, pleasures? What happened when the proportions changed unexpectedly? How flexible could one be and allow infiltration of one element into the space of another?

This all was in the last few pages. The last entry was carefully written, well spaced and short.

"After all, I am not where I am supposed to be, and should be. 'O' is is the only one who may understand it. The others may rightly feel I let them down and failed. There are no excuses other than the complexity of the human heart. For myself, I shall join the fight and give it the little I have."

He gave it his life, which to him wasn't much in the first part of the diary. Only the last few pages indicated a desire to be more than a tool, to dare to have an emotional life and fulfill himself other than within "the water business."

My mother brought the children back and had to leave. The sun was setting and I closed the shutters and windows.

"Is father coming home tonight?" Ofer asked.

"I doubt it. We may hear from him though. If he calls, I'll wake you up."

I fed them, watched them in the bath and tucked them in bed. Ofer wanted a sad story with a happy ending. I knew so many happy stories with a sad end, as many as the gravestones in the cemeteries and the beds in the hospitals. Only the summing-up of these sad ends, if the national history could be personified into "Once upon a time there lived a sad young man called Israel," could produce the sad story with the happy end he wanted.

We settled for Cinderella, my own version of it, and they were soon asleep.

And so was I when the phone rang.

Instinctively I looked at my watch. It was midnight.

"Is that Amalia?" a voice I couldn't place asked.

I think I didn't answer right away. Then I managed, "Something happened to Daniel!"

"Not to worry. He was wounded. No vital organs hurt. I'm taking him to Faid now, and he'll be flown to a hospital."

"Who are you? Is he alive?"

"I am David. Brigade commander. I had the pleasure of his company and the displeasure of his participation in the Suez battle. He is only wounded. That's the truth. We don't announce death on the phone these days."

"Please, can he be brought to the central military hospital, now?"

"I can try. I am a bad travel agent and it isn't up to me, but I'll try."

"You are telling me the truth, aren't you? Is it a head or spine wound?"

"No. And he is conscious and functioning. We've all seen much worse, so consider yourself lucky."

"I do. Thank you."

He hung up. The only thought in my head was *Daniel is alive. He is coming home.* The rest was mechanical. I tried to call Beni, but he wasn't there. I called the hospital's emergency ward.

Yes, they were expecting some helicopters, but weren't sure when. Not before an hour or so.

I put on my uniform and combed my hair. I called my mother.

"No, don't come over. The children will be all right. No, I don't know where he was wounded. Yes, he was conscious. No, I don't know what he was doing there. What does anyone do in a battlefield?"

Hell, I felt she was so scientific and cold. Void of hatred but not exactly flowing with love.

I touched Ofer's shoulder. He was a light sleeper.

"Listen, son, your father was wounded. He will be all right, and he is being flown to the hospital. Go back to sleep now. I'm going to meet him and return quickly. Take care of your brother."

"Will you be here in the morning?"

"Yes. Long before you wake up, and we'll visit father together tomorrow."

I doubted that it was wise of me to leave him with the anxiety and ignorance, but I was confident he could cope.

I stared in the mirror in the corridor. If Daniel were conscious and awake, I had to look my best. My eyes were shining, fully awake, but my face was drawn and pale. I applied the lightest touch of make-up to my cheeks and tried a cheerful smile. It didn't belong and I pulled a face and walked out.

Daniel was alive, and I could figure out now the process we all went through. We did expect the worst, and when it happened we were almost ready for it. Next to it everything was a valued gift, a safe return. Wounded, burnt, deformed—we've somehow been there in our subconscious, built up defenses, learned to live with it long before it happened.

I knew better than many others what injuries involved. I'd witnessed the pain, the despair, the shame and the pride. I knew the patience one needed until a total recovery was achieved, or adjustments were made to a lifetime handicap. Rina lost Amnon and watched her son, Uri, recuperate; Nadav's family slowly adjusted to his deformity, watched when the bandages were removed and were grateful to have him alive. The head and spine wounds were something else. More despair hung over the brain and head wounds ward than anywhere else. The fear of change in personality, of the unknown in the labyrinth of the gray matter, couldn't be easily overcome by patient doctors and kind nurses. Relatives of men shot in the head envied the amputees and the burnt. Even bad luck and misery had their degrees.

There was no activity in the landing site. It was a clear night, cold and moonless. In the little wooden hut a row of stretchers on wheels awaited the next landings and several youths were playing backgammon in a corner. They were high school students, doing their bit at night and studying during the day. Soon they too would be drafted and would believe that it could never happen to them. The miracle of healthy repression.

"I thought you were working days now," a doctor I knew greeted me.

"My husband was hurt. He may be flown here tonight."

"Suez, I suppose. What a bloody battle. About two hundred casualties, eighty or so dead. Is he badly hurt?"

"I don't know. They said he was conscious, we'll soon see."

"That's why you look so pretty tonight."

I blushed. It sounded horrible. Women should dress up for dates, to go dancing or romancing in the moonlight. Girls should pretty themselves to celebrate, to attract, to share a joy with someone. Here I was, my hair washed and eyes bright as if expecting a proposal, to welcome an injured man or a stretcher, attached to infusion tubes, bloodstained and defeated.

But he was alive, I kept saying to myself, and what

can be a better, more elementary cause for celebration than the knowledge that it's a hospital bed and not a grave he is coming home to. Two senior doctors joined us.

"Two helicopters left Refidim half an hour ago. They won't be long. Surgery is at standby, but we don't have a list. Head wounds were flown to Hadassah in Jerusalem, so I suppose we'll get the burns and orthopedic cases."

There was no use speculating. Daniel would soon be here and into surgery and all my unasked questions would be answered.

"You worked in Ward L?" the senior doctor asked me.

"I still do, but I am waiting for my husband here."

"I see. What happened to the unidentified case you had?"

"He died yesterday. We think we know who he was, though."

"Is Leibowitz still with you?"

"Left today, I think. Back to his New York practice."

"An excellent surgeon he was. Could use him in peacetime, too."

They chatted and sipped coffee until we heard the familiar sound of the circling and landing aircraft.

The teen-agers pushed the stretchers, turning their heads away from the gust of wind the rotors produced. The junior doctors followed, and I stood behind a couple of nurses, as close as I could without pushing my way to the stairs that touched the asphalt.

Two soldiers stepped down supporting each other and smiling. They walked into the hut and the next case was brought down with great care. It wasn't

Daniel, though I couldn't see the bandaged face well.

The following stretcher was carried out and laid on the mobile one. The limp left hand was hanging and the right part of the body was tightly bandaged. A blanket covered his body but the face was there, Daniel's face, unshaven and gray and tired, but the youthful eyes met mine and he even managed a smile.

I let them carry him in and I followed. I kissed his forehead and touched his lips.

"It's nothing," he whispered. "You needn't worry."

"Are you in pain?"

"Not unbearable. You are beautiful. How are the boys?"

"Waiting for you. They'll take you to surgery now. I'll wait until you are out and into a ward, then go home to them. You'll be asleep, and I'll be there when you wake up."

"You talk like a regular nurse." He smiled.

There was too much to say, so we said nothing more. The doctor examined him, almost casually, and he was wheeled on to surgery.

"The bullet has to be removed. Lucky to have it just where he did, above the vital organs."

I entered the surgery unit and sat in the waiting room. The strong neon light bothered me and I shut my eyes. It could have been a road accident, it was that unexpected. War was on, but mostly over, and Daniel was still at home two days ago, frustrated and tense. Everything that had happened before, happened to other people, not to us, and here I was, in the surgery waiting room and Daniel's chest had to be opened and an Egyptian bullet extracted from it.

Half an hour later an overtired surgeon I knew

told me it was over. Daniel was given a blood transfusion, and would be in the general surgery ward by morning. There was nothing more I could do there.

A pale dawn light was a good change from the neon light. The air was soft as feathers gently brushing against my cheeks. Everything seemed so precious. The new grass, the amber-colored leaves on the path, the chirping of sparrows. It's ridiculous, I thought. Now that my husband is in the hospital, has seen, once again, the horrors and felt the agony of another battle, I am at peace. Somehow I felt that ends met, that I had come to terms with our predicament. I wasn't "proud of him," I just felt that he had preserved his integrity in a way I could well understand. He wasn't careless with his life. The commitment he had was integrally bound with love for us. I wondered if the same could be said for Arik Berkov.

CHAPTER 14

Daniel didn't wake fully until late in the afternoon. My mother resumed her voluntary grandmotherly duty, and I sat in Ward N watching Daniel toss and turn in his sleep. All the intimacy in the world can't remove a slight sense of guilt when watching someone who isn't aware of being watched. Even more guilt when the person is Daniel who was always, I felt, a little bit on guard, never caught unprepared, never short of an answer, very careful at being as faultless as humanly possible. Here he lay, pale and unshaven, muttering in his sleep, moaning whenever a wrong turn hurt his shoulder, attached to a drip bottle and helpless.

He would have been happier to wake up alone, and I thought of leaving and waiting elsewhere. I never felt this way in Ward L. They were patients. Wounded soldiers who needed care or attention or urine bottles, and I was one of the girls in white. Most of them I would never see again.

Ward N was larger than L and less sterile. People were coming and going, and one of the rooms was reserved for civilians who couldn't wait for their ailments till the war was over.

When the nurse arrived with the afternoon tea, Daniel opened his eyes.

When did I last look at his eyes so closely? On our wedding day, in the maternity ward when Ofer was born, when this war started . . .

His dry lips held a smile, but the eyes were sad and void of luster. All the things I wanted to say seemed flat and trite or melodramatic and uncalled for, so I touched his good hand and burst into tears.

He watched me cry and watched me relax and wipe my eyes. I tried to smile and cried again.

The surgeon walked in, and I composed myself. He looked at the chart attached to the bed in the small single room and wrote something on it.

"You'll need a lot of rest. Don't try to do anything you don't have to. The pain should recede in a couple of days."

"How long do I have to be here?"

"Are you in a hurry? We don't know yet. The bullet by miracle missed the lung but the chest is a sensitive area. I'll see you in the morning."

The doctor left, and Daniel was relieved.

"I wonder how much they really know. So much seems guesswork and general trust. They are always so hopeful and optimistic that it makes you wonder."

He talked about the children. I promised to bring them over the next day. A nurse came in and helped him wash and shave. When she left, I told him about Arik Berkov. I told him all I knew, all I remembered of the diary and letters. I talked about the sad funeral, and I asked about the missing clues.

"I don't know whether to laugh or cry. Even the

banality of 'a small world' won't do here. Coincidence, maybe. Providence? I doubt it."

I wasn't sure what he was talking about.

"I went to look for him in Suez, after Gideon was wounded. The day he died, I was crawling into stinking rooms in a Suez suburb, with a flask of whiskey in my pouch, looking for him."

"He wrote about a job undone. He was in love, I think, a girl whose name began with O. He came for the holidays to be with her."

"Ofra. Very touching. Gideon could have been killed, so could I. One bit of information at the right moment could have saved many lives, if not more than that."

"What's the use, he is dead now."

"And he was the example of detachment, of duty above all. No human ties, no emotions, guided by logic and reason, a perfect operator.'"

"Which proves something?"

"Not really. It's rather ironic. I was determined to find him and convince him to live a normal life. Persuade him to let go of the codes and radio messages and clandestine existence, to find a home if not a homeland, and a girl, and join humanity. He beat me to it. Only the timing was foul. The timing and the end result."

"We could find Ofra? She may be somewhere waiting for him."

"Yes, you can find Ofra. She is on file somewhere."

He asked for the diary and the evening papers. Supper was wheeled in, and I watched him eat without appetite. He must have sensed my disappointment.

I felt as if a big wave had brought us together, momentarily, and another bigger one swept us apart.

"Amalia," he said very gently, "I love you. I have been somewhere, and I returned with many questions, which I have to answer, but I returned to you and the children, never to leave again."

He was being truthful, but it was also a way of saying he wanted to be left alone.

I bent to kiss him, and with one hand he pulled me toward him and kissed my lips as if we were the only two souls saved from a terrible catastrophe.

I respected Daniel's need for privacy, but I was hurt. He was a man in pain, not only physical pain, and he loved me and cared, yet he couldn't, or didn't choose to, share his pain. Yet there was something new between us, a new knowledge of what really mattered, a pact of the survivors, of those who have been through a terrible wreckage and have emerged hurt but together in order to start anew, reborn not as innocent babies but as disillusioned grown-ups trying to rekindle a fire from ashes and grow in its light and heat.

At home, I assured everybody that Daniel was well and that they could see him the following day. Only when my mother left did I call one of Daniel's friends and asked him to locate Ofra and have her contact me.

I called the hospital, talked to Shula, gave Avi my love and learned from the night nurse at Ward N that Daniel was asleep.

As I switched off the light the phone rang and an unfamiliar voice introduced itself.

"Ofra speaking, is that Amalia?"

"Yes. I really wanted to see you, it's not for the phone," I said clumsily.

"He is dead. I know. Arik is dead."

"Were you told about it?"

"I just knew, when he left on Yom Kippur, I knew. I even inquired once or twice, looked at some lists. When did he die? Was he in pain?"

"We buried him yesterday. He was unconscious in the hospital for a couple of weeks, and unidentified."

"Are you sure it's him?" she asked without hope.

"As far as we can tell. There are some things here which belonged to him. Perhaps you would like to have them. A book."

"Valéry? *Monsieur Teste*. I gave it to him."

"And a diary, sort of. Daniel, my husband, has it."

"I'll come tomorrow."

"Better to come to the central hospital. Daniel is wounded. He is in Ward N. I'll be there, too."

They don't announce death by telephone, I thought, yet I just did. She wasn't his wife or mother, just the girlfriend he came to live for and ended up dying for.

CHAPTER 15

The battle of Suez was the last battle. On Friday morning the newspapers devoted space to analysis rather than reports. The movie houses and theaters announced that performances were resumed, restaurants were reopened and the back page gave the new cease-fire maps in three colors.

There were no obituaries, as casualty lists were not made public yet. Couples whose weddings had been postponed announced the newly set dates.

Leading articles hinted at what was to follow. Things had gone wrong, and we'd have to find out where and why. What two or three weeks ago had been a terrifying supposition was now a certainty, still delicately handled. Having recovered from the initial shock, the long fingers and minds of the media started the search into the phenomenon of failure.

The media, and each of us privately, hesitantly, and with a touch of guilt.

I did the Friday morning shopping in a hurry. There were long lines at the market. Men began to return home on short leaves, and the shopping baskets boasted bottles of wine and beer, ingredients for baking and delicacies. It almost felt like back to normal, yet the same line of housewives, a month ago, had been in a different mood. Now above the chatter and the gossip there was an aura of unfathomable sadness, as if we all suffered a very personal loss.

I arrived at the hospital to find Beni and David in Daniel's room. For a brief second I felt like an intruder. I kissed Daniel and busied myself in a corner with some things I brought from home. They asked me to join them for coffee.

I had never met David and his language irritated me at first, but he was complimentary and scolded Daniel in a fatherly way that pleased me.

"My ex-chief from the service paid me an early visit," Daniel said. "He took the diary and the other things you left here. There was quite a scene. He takes responsibility for the bastard, he said, but he's going to find out exactly what happened and why."

"Ofra called. She is coming into town later."

"I don't envy her when they come around to questioning her."

"She is not at fault and he is dead, so what's the use?"

"The use is that next time you don't put your trust in one man only, and when you choose your men you make sure they don't run off on the eve of war to fuck someone a thousand miles away from where they are supposed to be," David contributed.

"It isn't that simple, is it?" Daniel countered. "And don't let us act as judges or prosecutors."

"The witch-hunt hasn't started yet. Soon the corporals will blame the captains, the captains will accuse the majors, and the generals will have to hide under the skirts of the politicians, and on it will go until we find rest." Beni wanted to go on but Daniel hushed him.

"We've won the war, so it can't be all bad."

"Ask the widows and the orphans whether we've won the war."

"There were widows and orphans in other wars."

"The victory was different. What went wrong here was much deeper. What failed was a concept, in historical terms. Not wrong tactics or one wrong move but a complete misconcept of where we were, what our enemy was like. What our and their capacity was. We'd gone slack all along the line and did we pay for it!"

They were all talking together. Daniel looked feverish, trying to put in a calming word, but I could see his mind was working faster than his tongue, which made him prefer silence after a couple of sentences.

"And this is only a rehearsal for what we are going to say and hear for a long time now," David summed up. "I am on my way to kiss the wife, then the girlfriend, then a few hours' sleep and back to sit under a palm tree until we are told that Mr. Kissinger is displeased with us there and we go back to where we started."

"Minus the canal," Beni sighed, and got up to leave, too. "I'm off to the prisoners' hospital. There is a colonel there I helped evacuate and promised to see."

"Love thy enemy," David snapped. "Better to visit him in the hospital than in the Chinese Farm."

"Better yet in Cairo." I tried to sound light.

"The day should come," said Daniel, ending the conversation, and the two men left, promising to return.

"Where are the children?" Daniel asked when we were alone.

"Mother will bring them after school. Ofer asked if you were in a cast, Rani did a drawing. I am glad they are familiar with the hospital."

Daniel was in pain and the nurse gave him an injection. "He shouldn't get excited," she said.

I walked over to Ward L. Avi was in a wheelchair in the dining room reading the papers.

"Hello, beautiful. How is Daniel?"

"Come and visit," I said.

He was cheerful and looked well. He was recuperating fast and began to be bored with the hospital routine.

"Julie called. She misses us all, she fund-raises for us and takes Hebrew lessons. She'll come for Easter, if I am still here."

"Will you still be here?"

"I suppose so. For a while. Help lick the wounds and join the choir of repenting idiots. Maybe this war will make me feel at home again. Starting from scratch is always a challenge."

"We're not exactly in ruins."

"Not quite, only morally."

"So you want to preach, you!"

"No. Just take advantage, if this place will again be something special."

I hated this kind of talk. The outsider giving a recipe, tasting the dish, criticizing, and "may come again" if we behave or produce something better next time.

I pushed his wheelchair to Ward N. He wanted to visit Daniel and I couldn't refuse.

I stopped at the doorstep as I heard voices. The door was open and on the chair next to the bed sat a girl in uniform. Her hair was auburn and very long and straight. She was heavy but not fat and I couldn't see her face. Her voice was soft, almost a whisper. I asked Avi to wait for me.

"Amalia, meet Ofra," Daniel said.

She turned her face to me. Her eyes were red and swollen, as if she had spent hours crying bitterly. There was something Slavic about her wide bone structure, like a country girl from the Ukraine, but her long fingers ended in well-manicured nails.

We shook hands and I mumbled some words of condolence.

"What a mess," she said, wiping another unwanted tear.

"He didn't suffer. He was unconscious."

"He suffered enough from the time the war started. Coma must have been a blessing for him. What a mess," she repeated.

"It's not your fault."

"I told him to go back. I said I'd wait till he left the service and returned to settle. He was like a blind person having a retina transplant and discovering the world. As if drugged, he had erased everything that wasn't us."

"When did you see him last?"

"Friday morning. Three weeks ago. I went home for Yom Kippur and he said he'd stay in his room. I was to return Sunday morning. When I came back he wasn't in. I didn't go into the room. The landlady said he had left, and that she would let me know when he was back. I received a postcard, a one-liner." She pulled one of the army distributed postcards from her handbag. The familiar handwriting read, "I was right but I apologize and I love you, Arik."

"And that's all," she said.

I remembered Avi at the door. I pushed him in and introduced everybody. Ofra chose to go out with me and we left the men chatting.

She wanted to know about his burns, his last days, the funeral. She would go to the cemetery now, she said. Before she left I felt there was something else she wanted to say.

"There is something that bothers you. Perhaps we can help."

"What a mess," she said. "I may be pregnant."

What was there to say? A mess it was.

"Don't do anything in haste. I'll be home later in the evening. You can come and spend the night and we'll talk more."

I saw her round figure disappear between the wards' flat-roofed buildings. A woman confused and ashamed and lonely. Everything seemed to happen for her too late.

Avi and Daniel were obviously talking about me. They stopped and smiled when I entered. I decided not to tell Daniel about Ofra, not until she made up her mind what to do next. There was no hurry.

When the children arrived, Daniel was asleep. They stood in the doorway and watched him, worried. Suddenly I saw Ofer's mouth twist as if about to cry, and it occurred to me that he thought Daniel was dead. I put on my brightest smile and cheerfully took them by the hand. "Here, let's wake up father, with a kiss, but carefully as he still has some pains."

He woke up gently and hugged them both. He touched their heads and faces and hands and comforted the little one who was on the verge of tears. In five minutes they settled on the bedside to tell and listen and I sat in the chair watching when I felt my mother's hands on my shoulders. She bent and kissed my head, something she hadn't done in so many years. I didn't dare look at her face to see how touched she was for fear of embarrassing her.

The Rabbi came into the room with sunset. I lit two candles and he talked to Daniel and the boys. The soldiers liked him for he never preached, just talked and laughed with a certain moral authority or self-confidence which we seemed to be short of these days.

He left and dinner was brought in. The boys shared Daniel's food and Rani fell asleep next to him on the bed while we all watched the evening news.

It's been only three weeks was a thought we all shared as the announcer went on summing up the recent events and political developments.

Friday, three weeks ago, we were on our way back home from the synagogue. My mother was in bed reading a book, Arik Berkov was alone in Beer-Sheba planning his life with Ofra, and hundreds of thousands of men couldn't for one minute imagine they'd be fighting a bitter battle the next day.

"Can I sleep here?" Ofer asked.

"No, son. Go home with mother and come back tomorrow." Daniel was exhausted and we took the boys and said good-night. Rani was asleep in my mother's arms, and Ofer clung to me like a baby as we walked into a chilly peaceful night.

My car was parked near Ward L. There was light in

some of the windows and someone playing a guitar in the large room. Professor Rothman came out of the ward and stopped to greet us.

"I heard about your husband. How is he?"

"Chest wound, the lungs are not hurt. He is lucky."

"Indeed. I suppose you'll be nursing him, but come and see us sometime."

"Of course. Thanks for everything."

"I should thank you."

He walked away, shoulders slightly bent under an unseen enormous burden.

I drove my mother home. Both boys were asleep in the back seat.

"Are you all right?" she asked when I parked in front of her apartment building.

"Yes. No worse than all of us."

"It's been a nightmare," she confessed.

"You are saying it? So cool and composed and organized."

"It's no use pretending. It helps for a while, then when it is shattered, it all breaks into a million pieces and even I don't manage to put them back in order. Will you manage with the boys?"

"Of course. Sleep well."

I had to wake Ofer up and carry Rani. I put them in my bed, changed and lay between then. Instinctively they cuddled and held me.

CHAPTER 16

I had the vague feeling that someone was gently rapping at the door. The doorbell hadn't rung but I got up and walked through the dark corridor and opened the front door. Ofra was standing there. She was no longer in uniform and her gray eyes were dry.

She apologized. She had gone to the cemetery, then got a hitch to the kibbutz where her parents lived and back to Tel-Aviv.

"I thought I'd consult with them but it was impossible. They are unhappy as it is. There were three funerals in the kibbutz. It's like in the family. They think of me as a rock of decency and morality, 'the good girl,' and I didn't dare say anything. Just changed and left."

I fried some eggs for her and made some coffee and we sat in the cold kitchen.

"I don't know what to do," she said.

"You should take your time. It's all too fresh and whatever you decide is going to affect the rest of your life."

"He returned for Rosh Hashanah. I don't know where from. We corresponded now and then, but his letters never indicated a deep attachment. Vague, uncommitted, an occasional touch of humor. Mine were more inviting. I wasn't sure whether he was fully employed by us. I wrote to England, kept inviting him to come over. I wrote him about the desert, Beer-Sheba, life in the university, the Sinai, my loneliness. I shared with him the love I have for places, nothing personal really.

"I returned from school one day and he was there. In the front garden of the house which I shared with two other students. I promised not to ask questions, not to tell anybody he was there. He said to introduce him, when I had to, as Arik, a newcomer from Britain. His Hebrew was amazingly good. I knew of a vacant room not far from where I lived, and he paid the rent in advance."

"Did he tell you he was on a job?"

"Only a week or so later. I took him with me to the kibbutz. He met my parents there, and told them he was an engineer thinking of settling permanently in Israel. They encouraged him. He said he was Jewish, which wasn't quite true, but I didn't interfere.

"He was on some sort of voyage of self-discovery. When he was alone he seemed tormented, struggling with something. With people, he listened. Most of the kibbutz elders are survivors of concentration camps. For him the Holocaust and the foundation of the state were inseparable. He kept referring to it.

"We made love. He was very gentle. He was very secretive, but I felt I was watching a process I couldn't define, like a snail sending feelers out, then its head, and then pulling back into the shell."

"Did he talk of his plans, did he contact anybody?"

"He said he would after the holidays. He was going

to look for 'the chief,' declare himself the victim of Eros and look for a job here. Once or twice he said he shouldn't really be here, it was wrong, and if something were to happen he couldn't forgive himself."

"You should have known better. You could have encouraged him to report in time."

"We were in love. Our world was walks in the wadi looking for desert plants, long talks about nothing and lovemaking. It all seemed innocent and calm and beautiful. We read Paul Valéry together, *Monsieur Teste*, the personification of total detachment. At first it amused him, and finally he felt sorry for him. I introduced him to Hebrew poetry, too."

"Sounds idyllic. Where did you think it was leading to?"

"It was short. Ten days was all we had. He said he kept a diary, his needs were minimal, there was something aesthetic in his behavior. Obesity produced decadence, he said. He loved looking at children. It was a new sensation he had, he said."

"He never mentioned Egypt?"

"Not really. He said once or twice 'across the border,' talking about vegetation, or food, or climate. He had money and bought books—history of Israel, geography, poetry. He said he should write to his mother, but he never did. I sound as if we spent years together, it was only ten days. The humanization of Mr. Berkov . . ."

"It's time to go to bed. I can't help you decide about the child, just remember that a child is not a monument to the memory of someone."

I made the bed in the living room, and she thanked

me and fell asleep instantly. It had been a long day for her.

The phone rang at four in the morning. It was Julie, from New York. She was with Leibowitz and they decided to call and find out how Daniel was.

"Bad news travels fast," I said, forgetting Avi talked to her in the morning. "He will be OK in a week or so."

"Is Avi staying?"

"You talked to him, didn't you, at a decent hour, too? How should I know?"

"Should I come over?"

"Julie, you are a big girl and you've made decisions in your life, so don't ask me at four in the morning to advise you."

"Sorry." And a pause, a long one for an overseas call. I had nothing to say and she was uncomfortable.

"I am sorry too. Give us some time. Don't judge and don't rush us, we are at some kind of a beginning again."

"Leib sends love," she said.

"Shalom now."

I hung up. I hadn't been very nice to Julie on the phone. This was no time for outside sympathy. It was the inside that needed an overhaul.

The children woke me up. They managed to wash and dress and were ready to leave to see Daniel. I opened the shutters to let in the light. The sky was deep blue, but the pavements were wet; it must have rained earlier, the wind sweeping all clouds away.

Before I left for the hospital, I woke Ofra up. For

a second she wasn't sure where she was but a smile followed.

"Thanks for last night."

"I'm off with the children to the hospital. Make yourself some breakfast. You can stay if you want to."

"I'll go back to Beer-Sheba. I have to be alone and figure it all out. I'll let you know what I decide. You've all been a great help. I'd like to have Arik's diary and the other things."

"They were taken from Daniel for inquiry. Someone will probably contact you, and when they are through with it, I suppose you can have it."

"I don't care for objects, but I thought, for the child . . ."

Saturday morning is slow even at the hospital. Food is warmed up rather than cooked, visitors arrive late, many with children, and some of the staff stay at home, on call for emergencies only. Whoever was able to walk or be wheeled went out to the lawn in front of the wards where visiting families opened picnic baskets and enjoyed the sunny day.

The past three weeks were the longest weeks the country had ever known, in the same way that the six days of the 1967 war were the shortest. The term "licking wounds" could easily be applied to the mood that prevailed this Saturday morning, but the depth of the wound and the eventual scar was yet to be assessed and treated.

Only as I stood in front of Ward L did I realize my error, but decided to go in anyway, hoping Daniel was still asleep.

The children stayed on the bench outside, looking

at a picture book, and I walked along the corridor. The last room was occupied now. A blond youngster was asleep in Arik Berkov's bed. His face was angelic and untouched, but bandages covered his chest and abdomen. The curtain was drawn and I stood there aimlessly. Beds are washed and scrubbed for a new patient, and even the smell in the room was different now. If Berkov left a trace somewhere, it wasn't here in room 7.

Avi was in his room having breakfast. I told him Julie called.

"I wasn't too charming to her, I'm afraid."

"Well deserved at four in the morning."

He wanted to know about Ofra. He found her vulnerable and attractive.

"When I am on my feet I may go to Beer-Sheba," he said half-seriously.

Nadav greeted me with a large smile.

"He's lucky, your husband. They say it was a bloody battle. Here, bend under the bed."

I did, to find a crate of tangerines.

"Take some for your husband and children. They are from the farm."

I left the ward with my arms full of green-orange fruit. He couldn't know it was my favorite.

The boys were impatient. We walked into Daniel's room together and found him propped up in bed. His hurt hand was resting in a cloth triangle tied around his neck.

"I can sit for a while. It's even less painful."

He was busy telling the boys a story when someone knocked on the door.

An elderly couple walked in. The man wore an

old battle-dress and held an envelope. He was past middle age and his face and hands were tanned and wrinkled. The woman was short and handsome, her hair in a bun and a woolen overcoat on her arm. One look at their red eyes told their story, the story of bereaved parents.

He helped her to the chair I pulled from the corner, and fumbling with the envelope he introduced himself and his wife.

"It was our dead son you carried from Suez. We buried him yesterday. In kibbutz Gal-on, where we live. Where he was born and grew up."

"I am sorry," Daniel said. "This is Amalia, my wife. And Ofer, and Rani, our boys."

The woman didn't try to hold back her tears. She stroked Ofer's head and he found refuge in my arms.

"We came to thank you," she said. "His friends told us you risked your life to save him, bring him home for burial."

"We never leave our dead behind. His friends said he was a wonderful commander. He was dead when we found him, but they said he fought like a lion."

The father sat down.

"Perhaps you won't understand it, but when they are brought home dead, it is still something. There is a boy missing in the kibbutz. His parents envy us. You see, we have a grave. A tombstone, a flower bed to tend in the cemetery."

"Do you have other children?" I asked.

"We have a daughter. She is about to get married. Her fiancé returned yesterday from the Golan. We had another boy, older than our Arik, that was his name—maybe you didn't know. He was killed in the Six Day War, in Jerusalem, near the Wall."

I was crying now and Ofer was frightened. The woman took some sweets from her shabby bag and offered them to the children.

"I always carry candies for children in my bag. An old, silly habit. Bad for the teeth, too."

The boys took the candies hesitantly, looking at us for permission.

The man opened the envelope.

"My son, Arik, was talented. He painted and drew. I brought some of his drawings for you. A small token."

He put two sheets of paper on the bed. They attracted the boys immediately for they looked like children's book illustrations at first. Bursting with lively colors, they were full of life and optimism, imaginary birds and flowers in lush landscapes.

"It is beautiful," Rani exclaimed.

"Thank you," I said, "but wouldn't you rather keep them?"

"We have others. We'd like you to have them."

They didn't want coffee. They had come a long way from Gal-on and were going back now.

"You are an officer," the man searched for words. "Tell me with honesty. What happened to us? How could it happen to us? Arik is dead, is it worth it?"

"Who can tell," Daniel whispered. "It's either never worth it, not one life, or you call it survival and believe that without the death and the agony and the pain there could be no life for us, for Ofer and Rani, for your daughter's children."

"It was different with our other son. He died for Jerusalem."

"And Arik died so we can keep Jerusalem."

"But this war was different," the woman said. Not aggressively, but with a conviction that was beyond dispute.

"True. We grew fat and clumsy. It's the old theme of the golden calf and the Ten Commandments. Somehow I feel they are bound together in our history, the material and the spiritual. We reach deep bottom in order to climb to great heights. If they hadn't sinned and worshiped the calf, then repented, and purified themselves, maybe there would have been no Ten Commandments. Jews in Germany stuck to their property and businesses, refused to believe anything could happen, and then came the Holocaust, followed by the foundation of the state. There was Sodom full of sinners, but Abraham emerged as a huge spiritual leader. The deluge produced Noah."

"Do you really believe the golden calf is broken and gone?"

"For a while. The young ones will have to build new foundations."

They wished Daniel a speedy recovery, kissed the boys and shook my hand.

"You should come and visit us. Gal-on is a beautiful kibbutz." We promised, and I accompanied them to the parking lot where a volunteer driver waited patiently.

"What have they done to deserve it?" I asked Daniel.

"It doesn't work like that. The innocent pay as much as the guilty. The price of belonging."

"In a week or so I think they'll let you leave.

Perhaps we should go somewhere quiet. Recuperate, think, be alone."

"We'll just go home."

There was love and care and trust in Daniel's eyes when he looked at me, and I couldn't lower mine. There was no hiding anymore. Layers had to be removed and we were exposed and naked again, back to an elementary beginning where nothing could be taken for granted.

ABOUT THE AUTHOR

Yaël Dayan, the daughter of General Moshe Dayan, Israel's Minister of Foreign Affairs, was born and educated in Israel. She joined the army during the Sinai campaign, rose to the rank of lieutenant, and wrote her first novel, *New Face in the Mirror*, during her military service. The book was a great critical success and was translated into fourteen languages. An extensive traveler and accomplished linguist, Miss Dayan wrote her next two novels, *Envy the Frightened* and *Dust*, in Greece. Her next novel was *Death Had Two Sons*, and her only work of nonfiction, *Sinai Diary*, was published in 1967. "The gifts of this young novelist are outstanding," comments Edmund Fuller. *Newsweek* has said that "Miss Dayan can evoke the physical world with striking and sensitive immediacy," and English reviews have praised her for "astonishing moral and technical toughness" and her "honest and moving" style.

Yaël Dayan is married to General Dov Sion and has two children, Dan, aged ten, and Racheli, seven.

Dell Bestsellers

- [ ] TO LOVE AGAIN by Danielle Steel $2.50 (18631-5)
- [ ] SECOND GENERATION by Howard Fast $2.75 (17892-4)
- [ ] EVERGREEN by Belva Plain $2.75 (13294-0)
- [ ] AMERICAN CAESAR by William Manchester . . . $3.50 (10413-0)
- [ ] THERE SHOULD HAVE BEEN CASTLES
  by Herman Raucher $2.75 (18500-9)
- [ ] THE FAR ARENA by Richard Ben Sapir $2.75 (12671-1)
- [ ] THE SAVIOR by Marvin Werlin and Mark Werlin . $2.75 (17748-0)
- [ ] SUMMER'S END by Danielle Steel $2.50 (18418-5)
- [ ] SHARKY'S MACHINE by William Diehl $2.50 (18292-1)
- [ ] DOWNRIVER by Peter Collier $2.75 (11830-1)
- [ ] CRY FOR THE STRANGERS by John Saul $2.50 (11869-7)
- [ ] BITTER EDEN by Sharon Salvato $2.75 (10771-7)
- [ ] WILD TIMES by Brian Garfield $2.50 (19457-1)
- [ ] 1407 BROADWAY by Joel Gross . . . . : $2.50 (12819-6)
- [ ] A SPARROW FALLS by Wilbur Smith $2.75 (17707-3)
- [ ] FOR LOVE AND HONOR by Antonia Van-Loon . . $2.50 (12574-X)
- [ ] COLD IS THE SEA by Edward L. Beach $2.50 (11045-9)
- [ ] TROCADERO by Leslie Waller $2.50 (18613-7)
- [ ] THE BURNING LAND by Emma Drummond $2.50 (10274-X)
- [ ] HOUSE OF GOD by Samuel Shem, M.D. $2.50 (13371-8)
- [ ] SMALL TOWN by Sloan Wilson $2.50 (17474-0)

At your local bookstore or use this handy coupon for ordering:

8 MONTHS A NATIONAL BESTSELLER!

EVERGREEN
by
BELVA PLAIN

From shtetl to mansion—Evergreen is the wonderfully rich epic of Anna Friedman, who emigrates from Poland to New York, in search of a better life. Swirling from New York sweatshops to Viennese ballrooms, from suburban mansions to Nazi death camps, from riot-torn campuses to Israeli Kibbutzim, Evergreen evokes the dramatic life of one woman, a family's fortune and a century's hopes and tragedies.

A Dell Book $2.75   (13294-0)